� The Mustang Men ✺

✳ The Mustang Men ✳

THORNE DOUGLAS

A FAWCETT GOLD MEDAL BOOK

Fawcett Publications, Inc., Greenwich, Connecticut

THE MUSTANG MEN

© 1977 Ben Haas

All the characters in this book are fictitious, and any resemblance to actual persons living or dead is purely coincidental.

ISBN 0-449-13918-2

Printed in the United States of America

10 9 8 7 6 5 4 3 2 1

✹ The Mustang Men ✹

❈ Chapter 1 ❈

His name was Shannon Tyree, and sometimes it seemed to him that he'd had nothing but trouble all his life—the cause of it always the same. It would seem, he thought, as his tired mount stumbled under him, that a man who had come as close to hanging as he had in California would finally learn. But no—he'd gone and done it again; and this time, with twenty Mexicans armed with antique guns and long, razor-keen lances after him, there was not much doubt that this would be his final lesson. They had fresh horses, plenty of them, and they could chase him in relays. Meanwhile, no matter how expertly he handled his own mount, it was reaching the end of its endurance. He could feel its barrel pumping beneath his thighs like an overworked bellows; it and he both were crusted with its lather, that dried instantly in the furnace wind off the

Llano Estacado. There were four cartridges left in his Henry rifle and two in his battered Remington revolver. So, he thought, reining in the exhausted dun, Doc was right.

Tyree swung down, a tall man in his late twenties, face burnt saddle-leather color by the sun, blue eyes fanned with wrinkles that came as much from smiling as from squinting, his long legs lean and hairpin-bowed from a lifetime spent on horseback. Since he could run no longer, he had to make a stand; and here on this kind of shelf, with a clump of waist-high boulders for cover, was as good a place as any. He ground-reined the horse, scuttled to cover behind the rocks, and as he sprawled behind them the voice of Doc Meredith seemed to ring in his ears again.

"Go straight?" Doc had grinned, punched him on the arm. "Yeah, until the first time you lay eyes on a hot-blood with perfect conformation and somebody else's brand. Then your hands'll start to itchin' and your mouth to waterin', and the next thing you know, you'll be on him with a necktie party right behind you. Face up to it, friend-boy. With some men it's booze and others it's women or cards. But with you and me—other people's horses will be the death of us!"

And so, Shan Tyree thought with more wryness than bitterness, Doc had known him better than he had known himself. Still, by God, not even Doc could blame him for the excitement that Mexican's big chestnut stud had kindled in him. That was the closest to a perfect piece of horseflesh he had seen in years. And with just a shade more luck he would have made it out of the *cibolero* camp with the stallion without being caught. The whole trouble was, he thought, managing a ghost of a crooked grin, you couldn't trust a Mexican. They just wouldn't let a good, honest horse thief go about his business in peace.

Then he sobered, squinting through a hole between the rocks. They were still coming, the heatwaves shimmering up off the rugged slope that was the rise of the caprock of the Staked Plains making them appear strange, vaporous, insubstantial, like riders in a nightmare. Sun glinted off of rifle barrels, lance points, as, seeing him go to ground, they spread out a little, taking their time now, knowing that they had him. Watching them come on, he felt the grudging admiration of one professional for another. Their mounts were superb—and the riders were probably some of the best horsemen in the world. In their business, they had to be. The *ciboleros* were professional buffalo hunters—and they ran down and killed their prey with lances instead of guns. Which, he thought, was the way they probably would take him.

They were still too far away for a shot. He waited, checking the action of the rifle, not bothering about the hand gun. It would be of no use for defense; he would probably not even draw it until the last, and then only to use one of its two loads on himself. Being hacked to death by spears was not the way he aimed to go.

God, it was hot here; that damned wind sucked the juice clean out of you! He mopped his face with his bandanna, begrudging the moisture it sopped up. *Doc*, he thought. *I should have listened to him when we split up* . . .

That had been in Silver City, Nevada, where the two of them were reasonably safe from the hangman's noose and

Shan Tyree had had time to think. He had, in fact, been thinking hard even before the posse had taken Big-nose Jackson, Fred Gilbert, and Fernando Ruiz and swung all three of them from a live-oak tree with no trial or ceremony, leaving the bodies dangling as a warning to all other horse thieves. Sitting in a bar in the Nevada boomtown, drinking bad whiskey that cost too much, what had been working in him surfaced. "Doc," he'd said, "it's over."

Doc Meredith, leaning back in his chair, arched pale brows. He had a round face and fine, silky blond hair that made him look like an overgrown baby, and he was almost always smiling, even in the tightest spots. "What's over?"

"All of it," Tyree lowered his voice. "It's just God's mercy that you and me weren't with Big-nose and the others when they was took. If we hadn't been scoutin' that bunch over near Mariposa, they'd have took us, too. Anyhow, we don't dare go back to California. They know we were part of the gang and if we do, we'll stretch rope like the rest did." He found a thin, black•cigar and lit it. "All I know is, I made up my mind when we cut Big-nose and the others down—what was left of 'em. That ain't the way I intend to end up. So I'm kickin' the game, I'm out of it. I'm goin' straight."

Doc set down his glass. "Now, wait a minute, friend-boy—"

"No, I mean it this time." Searching his own soul, Shan was surprised to find it true. "Look at us. Both of us damn near thirty, neither one of us what you'd call stupid in general, and when it comes to horseflesh and how to handle it, I bet there ain't a man in California can come within a mile of us. We've worked hard and we've risked our necks, and what the hell we got to show for it? Hang-nooses with our names on 'em back in California, my dun and your sorrel, our gear and blankets, and maybe sixty bucks between us. . . ."

"Fifty-eight after these two shots of rotten booze—"

"Fifty-eight, then. Hell's fire, we coulda worked for wages and come out better. Or mustanged on our own. Gone into the Army remount business, married, settled down—"

"Well, sure, friend-boy. And if a bullfrog had wings, it wouldn't bump its ass ever' time it hopped, neither." Doc's smile widened as he leaned across the table. "But what about the fun, the excitement, the big money we made and spent? And what about the horses—the good horses, the really fine ones that we couldn'ta afforded tryin' to git 'em straight, not in a month of Sundays, that we've rode and handled—and that belonged to us, for a little while, at least." He shook his head. "Go straight?" He reached across the table, knuckled Tyree's arm. "You can't help yourself! Oh, I know. You can walk past a thousand hammerheaded, broomtailed cold bloods and stay straight as a string! But then comes that one horse, that special horse . . . There ain't no point in fightin' it, friend-boy. And when you're made like we are, there ain't but one way to go—live fast, ride hard, and let the dice fall the way they roll. Now, we been together five years and we make a damned good team. This ain't no time to split up. I figured we'd head on east a ways, Colorado, maybe, or Injun Territory and get some boys together and—"

"No." Shan drained his glass. "I'm bound for Texas."

"Okay. Texas, then. Only they play a little rougher down there—"

Shannon Tyree looked at Doc Meredith. "Alone," he said. "I figured to make Texas alone. They say it's a good place to start over."

For the first time, Doc's smile went away. Then, despite the round face, the silky hair, he did not look so much like a baby. Then it was easier for Shan Tyree to remember that while he himself had never killed a man, Doc could have claimed four notches on his gunbutt. "Now, friend-boy . . ." Doc began. But his eyes met Tyree's and his voice faded. After a moment the smile came back, he shrugged. "Well, if that's the way it is, I can't stop you. All I can do is wish you luck."

"Doc . . ."

"Hell, skip it. You want one thing, I want another. Just because we're the best friends each other ever had don't mean we're married to each other. Now— Let's have another drink, and then we'll divvy up the money."

The Mexicans down there on the slope were closer now, would soon be within good rifle range. Still mounted—they did everything on horseback—they came warily, using the lay of the land, every bit of cover there was. Shan Tyree's hands sweated on the rifle. Soon he was going to have to kill his first man. But it was a case of have-to. He just couldn't lie here with bullets in his gun and let the *ciboleros* spear him to death, no matter how much he might have it coming—

He had bumped into their camp two days ago, east of here on the buffalo range: a dozen big-wheeled, primitive wagons corralled to make a fort, rack upon rack of fresh-killed meat drying in the sun, barrel upon barrel of buffalo tongues being laid down in salt. At first he had been wary; almost, he had ridden around them. But they were the first other humans he had seen in ten days of travel across this endless land, and the smoke of their campfires, the laughter of their women, and the whinnying of their superb *caballada* drew him irresistibly.

Next to Indians, they were the wildest, fiercest bunch of people he'd ever met. Whole families of them, up from Chihuahua, the men went out every day on buffalo surrounds, mounted on fast, brave, well-trained horses—and because guns and ammunition were too expensive for all the killing they had to do, they ran down the fat young cows, riding hard alongside, risking their own destruction in the stampeding herd, and rammed home razor-keen lances with eight-foot, even twelve-foot, shafts. Later the jerked meat and salted tongues would bring premium prices in northern Mexico, where it was a staple of the diet.

All this he learned after they accepted him. At first they had not been happy to see a *gringo*, but when it turned out that he was fluent in their language, albeit with a different accent, and as adept at their kind of horsemanship as they, and maybe even more so, their wariness yielded to the instinctive hospitality and graciousness so much a part of the makeup of the ordinary Mexican. Only with the one called Gregorio Velasco had there been any trouble.

Velasco was not their leader, but he wanted to be; a tall man with a drooping black mustache and a long scar down one side of his face. Clad like the others in leather, he was one of the few who affected any ornamentation:

braid on his sombrero, silver conchas on his pants-legs, big Chihuahua spurs, though his fine chestnut stallion never required their touch. Full of pride and arrogance, he swaggered through the camp like a cockerel, making no secret of his contempt for *norteamericanos* in general and *Californios* in particular. "So. That's a horse?" he'd sneered, running his eyes over Tyree's dun. "Where I come from, we'd call it a burro." Velasco had spat. "Gringo-trained, and ruined, completely ruined."

Shan Tyree was not a man who lost his temper easily, and he'd only grinned and nodded. In a way, he agreed with Velasco—the dun was a good, sturdy animal with speed and bottom, but it had been broken by an American bronc stomper long before Tyree had stolen it—a few sacking-outs, a couple of bridlings and saddlings, and then all the fight ridden out of it in two or three fierce sessions, after which it was considered a trained horse. By contrast, if Tyree himself had had the breaking of it, he'd have handled the animal precisely as Velasco himself would have, using a hackamore to preserve the fineness of its mouth, taking weeks, not days to make a working horse out of it. And when he'd finished, it would have been instantly responsive to the faintest signal of rein or knee or heel, able to stop on a dime from a dead run, then pivot, back up or crabwalk, whatever was demanded of it. After such training, horse and rider became part of one another, a single unit—but it was a process that took time, and time was something American ranchers, unlike Mexican *ciboleros*, counted as money.

"Now I'll show you a *real* horse," Velasco said and whistled softly. That was when Tyree saw the chestnut stallion for the first time. And promptly fell in love with it and knew he had to have it.

The animal came from behind a wagon, crested neck arched, sleek hide gleaming in the sun, and somehow it seemed to float across the ground as it ran to its scar-faced master. It was such a horse as he had never seen before and perhaps would never see again, with the blood of the Barb showing plainly in it and tall and strong and supple, flawless from nose to tail. Unsaddled, unbridled, it nuzzled Velasco and he leaped to its back. Then, using only the pressure of his knees, he put it through its paces. And Tyree watched, mouth dry with an old, familiar greed. Before Velasco had dismounted, grinning triumphantly, he was already planning how to steal it.

"You see? No *norteamericano* could ever train such an animal!" Velasco's grin was mocking as he dismounted.

"I could," Tyree said.

Velasco only laughed, spat, turned away. *All right, you cocky sonofabitch,* Tyree thought, the decision firm within him now. That contemptuous dismissal of his horsemanship had been like a slap across the mouth.

So, patiently, fitting into the camp and its operations as best he could, he spent the next twenty-four hours sizing up his chances. If he could only stay long enough with the buffalo hunters, he was bound to have an opportunity. And, watching Velasco, any twinge of conscience quickly faded. Even among his own people the man was feared and hated. Priding himself on his ability as a knife-fighter, Velasco had an almost insane readiness to use his blade in the most minor of disputes. Worse, he was the only womanless man in camp—and no man's wife or daughter was safe, Tyree caught the rumor, from Gregorio Velasco.

But none of that made it easier to steal the stud. The *ciboleros* lived in constant fear of Comanches, and each man kept his best mount tied to a wagon at night in case of a raid. Velasco slept almost under the hooves of the big chestnut, bringing it in at twilight after it had grazed. There was only one way to get it—Indian style. About two in the morning, when men slept most soundly, Tyree would have to make his play, sneak across the camp, cut the stallion's *mecate*, mount and ride before anybody knew what was happening. Given the slightest head start, there was no doubt about the stallion outrunning any other horse in camp.

He was careful that night to pay no particular attention to the stud after Velasco had tethered it. But Velasco was paying attention to him. As they sat around the campfire after a meal of roasted hump ribs and tortillas, Velasco's dark eyes sought him out. "Hey, *gringo*." His tone made the insulting term more so. "That's a pretty nice rifle you've got on your saddle, that Henry, that repeater. What'll you take for it, eh?"

Tyree's eyes flickered to his own mount, saddled, bridled, tied to a cart shaft, and the Henry in its scabbard, the best, most modern long-gun in the whole *cibolero* camp. He made a joke of his answer. "Trade it to you for the chestnut stud."

Everybody laughed and Velasco snorted. "*Gringo* talk, all right, all words, no brains. Now be serious. What'll you take for the gun? I want it."

"Sorry," Tyree said. "It's not for sale."

Velasco studied him a moment, silently. "Everything has its price," he said at last. He got casually to his feet. "Even a man's life."

There was silence around the fire. Slowly Shannon Tyree arose, no threat in his posture, but his right hand dropping casually close to his holstered Remington. "Why," he said, "I suppose you're right about that. I have seen some lives sold very cheaply." He was good with a gun, fast; Doc had taught him that, and Doc was one of the best; and he had learned on his own that a willingness to fight when challenged saved a man more fighting than it led to.

It did, now. There was a rusty old handgun of uncertain make jammed in Velasco's sash, but cold steel was his specialty, and he knew the American would never let him get close enough to use it. His eyes locked with Tyree's for a moment. Then, coolly, he shrugged and turned away. Later Tyree saw him sitting by the tethered stud, whetting his lancepoint on a stone.

Meanwhile the other *ciboleros* looked at him with growing hostility. They might hate and fear Velasco, but he was one of their own; they had not liked a *gringo* facing him down. So his welcome was worn out anyhow, Tyree told himself, and it had to be tonight. He waited a few disarming moments, then slipped into his blankets next to the tethered dun. Before long, the fire had died to a pale red glow and everyone except the night guards outside the corralled wagons was asleep.

Time crawled by. Coyotes and wolves fought in the distance over the remains of the last kills made by the *ciboleros*. The closely guarded horse herd outside the wagon circle grazed peaceably. Tyree rubbed tobacco in his eyes to keep awake as billions of stars wheeled across the enormous sky. Staring at them, he wrestled with his own conscience. *Like a goddam drunk*, he thought. But the lust for that stallion, the need to have it, was too strong to be conquered. He despised, hated, that weakness in himself, but there was nothing he could do about it. And now it was time . . .

He raised himself slightly; no one stirred. The stallion was only thirty yards away, across the corral of wagons. Velasco seemed to be sleeping quietly in his blankets. Tyree opened his pocket knife, grasped the rifle, made sure his Remington was in its holster. He would have to leave a lot behind—but he would sacrifice the dun, his bedroll, all his gear for the chestnut.

He had already removed his spurs, lest they jingle. Now, in one quick dash, he came up, running soundlessly toward the tethered stud.

Then a sound behind him made him halt and whirl. A dark shadow had stepped from behind the wagon to which his dun was tied, had thrust down hard into his empty bedroll with a lance.

That one frozen instant cost Tyree the stallion. Velasco's grunt of surprise as the lance head penetrated only blankets was loud in the silence. Then the Mexican had turned, seen Tyree standing there, and, without hesitation, lance head out, had charged.

Instinctively, Tyree raised the rifle, fired. Velasco's leg went out from under him; he pitched forward on the ground, yelling in a pain-wrenched voice, "Help! The *gringo* bastard tries to kill me!"

The night guards were already jumping between the wagons into the circle. Others came up out of their blankets. Blocked off from the stud, Tyree wasted no more time on the fallen *cibolero*. Instinctively he ran toward his dun, slipped the reins, hit the saddle without touching stirrup. "He tried to steal my horse!" he heard Velasco scream behind him. Then the dun had leaped a pair of cart-shafts, was thundering through the darkness, headed west. Tyree bent low in the saddle, but there were no following shots. Only cursing, confusion, and then the drum of hoofbeats as men mounted, rode, in prompt pursuit.

And now, he thought, watching them come up the slope, they had him. And the irony of it was that, had he been an honest man and not a horse thief, he'd already be long dead. He and Velasco had been playing the same game, his prize the stud, Velasco's his guns, gear, and vengeance for the facing down. Maybe they were both getting what they deserved.

Anyhow, his life hung in the balance now, he must do *something*. Still, he had no quarrel with those men who stalked him and who had given him their hospitality. His mind worked swiftly, searching for an out. Then it seized the one chance he had. . . . Tyree opened fire.

The first slug raked a horse's rump, sent it plunging. The second plowed a furrow across the flank of another animal and it too went mad with pain, suddenly uncontrollable. The other *ciboleros* stared, halting their advance, and Tyree somehow found a grin. These were brave men who risked their lives every day and put little value on them. But what they did value was their horses—and now, levering another shell into the chamber, he roared his warning.

"Go back!" he bawled in Spanish. "I have no quarrel with you! But if you don't go back, I'll kill your horses, every one of them!" For emphasis, he fired again, and another mount creased by a bullet whirled and went to bucking.

Tyree held his breath. They had no way of knowing the threat was doubly empty. He would almost sooner kill a man than a horse, but they could not know that—and could not know, either, that he was down to only three rounds of ammunition for rifle and six-gun combined. The sun beat down on him ferociously as he waited, bathed in sweat. Then his pulse began to hammer with the rise of hope.

They were indeed dropping back. He watched as they turned their horses, on which the livings of themselves, their wives and children, hung. Riding hard, they put themselves out of rifle range, gathered in council far below, only tiny dots in the shimmering heat. There was much argument among them; some, maybe most, would be insisting Velasco was not worth it . . . maybe.

The council went on for a long time. Then two men detached themselves from it, and Tyree swore. That pair of hotheads would not give up. While the others held back, they came charging up the slope, riding superbly, low in the saddle, horses zig-zagging, lances at the ready. Tyree sucked in breath. Well, he would have to do it. Carefully he lined the Henry, selecting the worst of the pair of horses. Hoping he had the proper lead, he squeezed off his last round for the rifle.

The horse, a lathered bay with a fine and gallant stride, went down as the gun roared. Its rider pitched from the saddle, and his head struck a rock and neither he nor the animal moved again. The other *cibolero* whirled his mount, dashed for his fallen comrade. Tyree drew the Remington, sent a bullet down the slope, and missed. Then he swore in admiration as the Mexican leaned from the saddle at a dead run, seized the slack of his fallen comrade's jacket, dragged him up. Reviving, the horseless *cibolero* caught a stirrup leather, and with a twist of his body was up behind the saddle. Tyree fired the last shot in the Remington to speed the double-riding pair on their way as the man in the saddle turned his mount, racing it back down the slope.

"And that," he said aloud, "is the last button on Gabe's britches." If they still wanted him, all they had to do was come and get him. He could only wait and hope he'd proved that the game was not worth the candle.

His throat was raspy dry; he swigged briefly from his canteen. There was not a lot in it, and the single swallow of tepid fluid was unsatisfying. Damn it, were they going to jaw all day down yonder? Time crawled by as the knot of men on the bench argued.

And finally made their decision. Shan Tyree watched tensely as they spread out into line. The sun glittered on the heads of uplifted lances. Then they spurred their horses, and Shan's breath went out in a long, whistling gust. For they were not charging again—they were turning tail, galloping off toward the east, back to camp. Weak with the release of tension, he leaned back against a rock. *So*, he thought. *They figured one horse was already too much to pay for Velasco's leg and honor. . . .*

He sat there for several minutes, then wearily arose. He was still not out of the soup, not by any means. He looked up at the brassy sky as he gathered up the tired dun's reins. Alone in Comanche country, with not a cartridge left to his name, a worn-out horse and not much more water in the canteen than spit in his mouth. He surveyed the jumbled land towering above him. Well, at least he was alive. Mounting, he let the dun pick its own way up the slope, and by nightfall he was over the caprock's rim and on the vastness of the great, treeless grassland that men called the Llano Estacado—the Staked Plains.

❈ Chapter 2 ❈

He had once gone out on a fishing boat from Monterey, and when land had been left far behind, the sea had been like this—enormous, rising and falling in continuous swells, the wind unceasing. As on the ocean, a man could see for miles, clear to the horizon; the only difference was the giant yucca that studded the plains, the cholla, and an occasional clump of mesquite which had sunk its taproots dozens of feet beneath the surface of the ground in search of moisture. He had the odd feeling that he was a man adrift at sea, the horse beneath him his small boat; and it was a sensation of awesome, terrible loneliness. And he began to wonder if he would survive. The presence of game—deer, antelope, buffalo—was a mockery, for he had nothing with which to kill it. And there were sharks, too, on this sea of land—the Comanches—and just as dangerous as any man-eaters of the deep.

Still, he was not a man whose spirits could stay down for long. Hope came easier to him than despair, laughter easier than a frown. He was not accustomed to borrowing trouble, or looking farther ahead than the next frolic, fight, or bottle—or the next raid on somebody's horses. What was past was forgotten, what lay ahead not worth worrying about until it happened. That was why he and Doc had hit it off so well.

All the same, traveling across this sort of terrain gave a man an awful lot of time to think, remember, and ask himself what he was doing here. And some of those thoughts, some of those memories, some of the answers to that question, were not much fun to dwell on. Anyhow, it all came down to horses. And to *Tio* Alvaro.

His love of horses was, he supposed, inherited. His father had been a trader in them, and a racing, gambling man, who always had a string of fast hotbloods to match in contests on Sunday at the mining camps. His mother dead before he could remember her, he had traveled the whole length of California countless times with Mason Tyree, and, as he got older, had ridden as jockey in the match races that provided the older Tyree with most of his income. But in a sense, *Tio* Alvaro had been his real father.

Rumor had it that the old man had once ridden with Joaquin Murietta and Three-fingered Jack. If so, those days were long behind him. Mason Tyree's only hired hand, *Tio* Alvaro had taken responsibility for the Tyree horse herd and for Shan himself while his father roistered and gambled in this camp or another. And it had been

Tio Alvaro who had taught Shannon Tyree *la Jineta*, the old *Californio* style of horsemanship. "Patience," he had said. "First of all, patience. To train a fine horse is like gaining the love of a good woman; it cannot be done overnight, and strength counts for nothing, for one cannot beat a woman into loving one or a horse into learning. If you try that, both will betray you in the end." And so, during those years of wandering, he had soaked up everything *Tio* Alvaro knew about horses almost through his pores. Long before he could read or write, he knew precisely how much pressure on the noseband of a hackamore would hurt the tender nerves of a young colt; the logic behind the use of the spade bit, which was directly the opposite of what most Anglos supposed, and a hundred other tricks of *Tio* Alvaro's trade, all of which the old man made him practice. He learned as well to become an expert with the sixty-foot rawhide riata, to throw all the horse-catching loops with nearly unerring accuracy. And because in the end any horse worth his salt would buck somewhere along the line, he learned the hard way to ride anything with hair.

He was fifteen when Mason Tyree took one drink too many and tried to outdraw a professional gunman in an argument over a sidebet on a race. After the burial of his father, he and *Tio* Alvaro drifted south, breaking horses for the big spreads around Los Angeles, which, mostly worked by *vaqueros*, wanted mounts trained in the Spanish style. One day a rambunctious stud crushed Alvaro against a boxstall wall, breaking almost everything inside the old man's body, and then Shan Tyree, at eighteen, was on his own, his father's hot, reckless blood beating hard within him and the deadly infection already settled in him—that need to own, possess, fine horses.

Still, he might never have fallen into the horse thief's trade if he'd not met Doc Meredith in San Bernardino.

Only a couple of years older than himself, Doc had been in the Civil War, assistant to a veterinarian in the Union Cavalry and on occasion an active combat trooper, too. Like Tyree, he loved fine horses, and the war had sparked within him a restlessness, a recklessness that matched Shan's own. Together, for a while, they broke horses under contract, but not for long. Doc was sick, fed-up, with the monotony of working for wages: "God damn it," he said, "I didn't live through the war to spend the rest of my life as somebody's blasted peon. Me, I aim to make some money, big money, and make it fast. Because, friend-boy, a man don't pass this way but once, and he'd better enjoy hisself while he can. I've seen too many men cut down before they had a chance to even live. Me, I may go young, but before I go, I'll by God have some fun. And fun is what you don't have unless you got some money. And money I know how to get— plenty of it, quick." He leaned forward across the table in the cantina. "Now, listen. I know some people up near San Luis Obispo that'll pay good money for broke geld- ings—and they ain't a bit particular about the brands they wear. I figure you and me together could handle about twenty that far—and the pay-off'll be three, four times what we could make in a coupla months' hard work. What'ya say, friend-boy? You want in?"

Tyree reined up the dun, eyes searching the surround- ing vastness warily. Seeing nothing, he let the animal move on, having its head. They were going to need water soon, and the horse could locate it more quickly and surely than himself.

That day in the cantina, he thought, it could have gone either way. The pause before giving Doc his answer was the pivot point of his life. He knew which horses Doc meant, which pasture they were in, and how long it would take for them to be missed—and something leaped within him, the lure of adventure, the need to gamble, and that was strong enough to overcome even the scruples about another man's stock that *Tio* Alvaro had drummed into him. He had looked at Doc for one long, steady moment, and then he'd grinned. "Why the hell not?" he said.

And that first time it had been easy, absurdly so. They'd quit their jobs, pretended to drift out of the county. By the time the horses had been sold at the place near San Luis Obispo, they still had not even been missed on their home range. The only thing dismaying about the whole experience had been how quickly the money they'd made had melted away. But now they knew how to get more—anytime they wanted it.

He and Doc made a good team; even after they threw in with Big-nose Jackson and his gang, they were always a little bit apart, always working off somewhere on their own—which was why they had not stretched hemp with the others. And once you got in the habit of taking what you wanted whenever you wanted it, it was harder than ever to pass up a fine horse that belonged to another man. Like a woman, you might not want to keep it forever, but you craved the enjoyment of it before you passed it on to someone else.

But all that was over, now, done with, had to be. He

swore it. This last fiasco had taught him his final lesson. If he ever got off this damned lonesome highground and back to civilization, he'd—

The dun snorted, fell, and there was sound like a breaking stick. Pitched free, Shan Tyree hit the ground hard, rolled. As the horse's pain-filled whinny rang in his ears, he knew what had happened even before he sat up, saw it trying to rise, finally making it with its off foreleg dangling limply.

Tyree's groan of despair was as much for himself as for the horse as he scrambled to his feet. The old badger hole had been completely grassed over; the horse had stepped into it blindly, stumbled wearily. Now, Tyree saw with sinking heart, the cannon bone was cleanly snapped.

The horse snorted with pain, whickered. Tyree looked around at the endless reaches of the Llano Estacado, at the merciless sky overhead. Then talking gently, soothingly, he went to the ruined horse. His presence seemed to give it comfort and it rubbed its sweaty head against him.

And not even one bullet in my gun, Tyree thought bitterly. "All right, old son," he said aloud, softly, scratching the knot between the horse's ears. "I'll do what I can, but it's bound to hurt you some more." Slowly and carefully he unsaddled. The horse stood quietly watching him, but it was shivering with the pain. Unlatching his riata, Tyree shook out a small loop, slipped it around the horse's neck, far down to the shoulder. Then he took out the pocket knife and opened it, testing its blade on his thumb. It was slightly dull; he spat on a small rock and whetted it until he was satisfied that it held the best edge he could put on it. Then, with a quick yank of the riata, he pulled the horse over; it landed hard, but on its near side, so that there was no impact on the injured leg. Instantly Tyree was sitting on its head to keep it from rising. His fingers probed for the main artery; then, as quickly and as deftly as he could, he cut the horse's throat.

Its dying was not something he wanted to watch, and he turned his head away while it struggled, hoofs flailing. He tried not to hear the sounds it made. Presently, when it lay lifeless, he arose. After a while he dared look at its corpse. "You first," he said bitterly. "Me next, I reckon." His own voice sounded loud and harsh to him in the silence of this empty land.

Freeing the riata, he coiled it. Then he slipped the bridle off, draping it around the saddle horn. Hefting that gear, he carried it well away from the dead horse; likely he would never come back to claim it, but if he did, he did not want it ruined by the wolves that inevitably would fight over the carcass. He slipped the coiled rope around his shoulder, slung the canteen with its few remaining swallows of water, took the Henry rifle from its scabbard. He would need food soon, and he thought about cutting some meat from the horse, but his gorge rose at the idea. He would also need a blanket, his own having been left in the *cibolero* camp, so he used the saddle strings to tie the saddle blanket in a roll. Wet and sodden as it was, it would dry soon enough in this furnace wind.

Laden with all that gear, he turned south and began to walk, bound he knew not where, without food, ammunition, or water for more than a few hours. This time there was no rising of spirits, no optimism in him. A man on foot out here was a man already dead; that cracking sound of the dun's leg breaking was, he knew, as sure a death sentence as any judge could pronounce. *If I had just gone on to Colorado with old Doc* ... But *ifs* were no use now; he must focus all his attention on survival.

He had lived his life nearly entirely in the saddle; neither his legs nor the tight, high-heeled, custom-made boots were made for walking. Within a pair of hours, his legs were cramped, his feet rubbed raw. At last he sat down, used the knife to slit the boots in several places; that helped a little, but not very much. Panting, lips dry and cracking from the hot wind, he shook the canteen, forced himself not to drink. Slipping a pebble under his tongue, he wearily arose, went on, under a sun that seemed pasted in the sky, across a grassland wholly devoid of shade.

At nightfall, he allowed himself half the water in the canteen, wrapped himself in the crusty, now-dry saddle blanket, and shivered through the darkness, not daring to build a fire for fear it would attract Comanches. The wind, once so hot, now blew chill across the flats, with nothing to break its force. Coyotes and wolves yapped and howled a symphony from every quarter of the compass. He must, at last, have drowsed, for when he wakened, the sun was coming up.

Desperately thirsty, he drank the last of the water in the canteen, rolled the blanket, and with every muscle protesting, set out again. If he could get far enough south of the range of the *ciboleros*, he could once more cut eastward, perhaps get off these plains into country where there was at least a chance of finding water. Of course, there was water somewhere up here, too, had to be, or else the game and Indians could not have lived here. But waterholes would be few and far between, and it would be sheer luck to happen on one. Anyhow, in broken country, a man could hide from Indians; out here, coverless, he stood out like a sore thumb.

By midmorning the wind, hot and dry once more, had sucked from his body the scant moisture of his final drink. His vision blurred; his stomach growled with hunger; his tongue was starting to swell in his mouth, and each step on raw feet was a separate agony. Still, driven by something within him that would not quit, he kept on. His mind gradually slipped all its gears, began to drift; he had dreams and nightmares while still awake. By noon, he collapsed in the scanty shade of a giant yucca with a treelike stalk. After an hour's rest that was no refreshment, the idea came to him that it was foolishness to get up, keep on. This was as good a place to die as any. And it need not be slowly. He could use the knife on himself, as he had on the horse.

Instead, he scrambled up, set out again into the shimmering emptiness. For a long time now, he had not even seen any game, which meant, of course, that he was walking away from water, not toward it. With the last power of decision remaining to him, he turned from south to east, *ciboleros* or no. After a while, he threw away the blanket; its weight seemed too enormous to be borne. But he would not let go of the rifle nor the coiled riata around his shoulder.

Within two hours he was falling down. He was not even aware of its happening until he found himself on his knees or sprawled flat in the shortgrass. Somehow, he always managed to get up, but the knowledge was in him now that sooner or later he would fall and lack the strength to rise. Then it would be over.

But for now he lurched on.

And then he saw the mesquite sprout.

Only a seedling, it was hardly more than a foot in height. Yet it was the first mesquite he had seen since yesterday, and his mind struggled with the significance of it. It had to mean something, that one dot of greenery in all this sun-dried dun-colored land. He stared at it for a long time before a voice seemed to ring in his brain—that of old *Tio* Alvaro, who had not spent all his life in California. He had never admitted it, but after the break-up of the Murietta gang, he must have fled eastward for a while; he had known these high plains and the wildlife on them.

"It is the horse that carries the mesquite seed," Alvaro's voice in his brain said. "The wild horses eat the beans and drop them in their dung. And so, when we were mustanging out there, and we found the mesquite growing in a place where it was a rarity, we knew a horse had brought it there, and that there were mustangs in that country."

Horse. Mustang. The two words were like a drink of water, clearing Tyree's head. He had seen none so far, nor any sign of them, but yes. Out here on these grasslands, there must be mustangs. He'd heard stories of the vast troops of wild horses in Texas, New Mexico, and Arizona, and of course Nevada had them, too. Somehow hope rose in him at the very thought of horses, though how a man on foot could catch a wild mustang, he had no idea. He'd heard of Indians walking them down, but he was no Indian. . . . Still, there was renewed energy as he lurched on, and now he watched the horizon as well as the ground in front of him with purpose.

Only twenty minutes later, he found them, the fresh tracks overlying old ones—and made by unshod horses. Tyree's heart kicked. Good God, there must be half a hundred in the band, maybe more, and it could not have been more than a few hours since they had passed this way: scattered dung still fresh told him that. The tracks led west, exactly opposite the direction he had chosen, but instinctively he reversed his course. Horses—they had to drink. And there was nothing to lose by hoping this trail would lead him to where they watered. They were, judging from the sign, certainly moving purposefully. If they had already drunk, they would have been ambling, straying, grazing. So surely they were bound toward water. Of course, it might be ten, fifteen miles away, a distance he knew he had no hope of making. But it could be closer, too—and it was the only chance he had.

Following their trail, he lost all track of time or distance. It might have been an hour, it could have been two or three; it might have been two miles or half a dozen, he never knew. All he knew was that just as his newfound strength seemed ebbing, just as despair rose in him once more, he heard it, borne on that furnace wind—a strange shrill screaming, a ferocious grunting which his mind identified at once: the sound of stallions fighting.

"Ahhh . . ." Tyree shook his head to clear it, licked his dried and blistered lips. Now there was fresh vigor in his pace as he hobbled on. At last, topping a rise, he saw them.

Below, the land dropped into a narrow, rugged valley seamed with a thread of green. Where the valley headed in a steep ridge outcropped with rock, a broad pool of water glinted in the sun, and there the wild bunch drank. A few mares grazed; most watched with pricked ears the combat of the two mustang stallions almost as the water's edge.

The big roan was at least ten years old and defender of the herd. The bay could not be more than six, in his prime, and, Tyree guessed, the challenger. Panting, Tyree dropped flat in the grass, watching.

It was a sight he'd often seen, one always awesome. When stallions fought for mares, they gave no quarter; before this was over, one would have to run or die. Within a minute, Tyree knew it must be the older roan.

The bay was coming at him hard, remorselessly, with chopping teeth that sought the jugular, flailing hooves. Two huge animals, wholly wild, each weighing over half a ton slammed together time and again, screaming their rage. The bay's teeth raked a long gash in the roan's crested neck; the roan pivoted, flailed out with both hind hooves. Like lightning, the bay dodged, reared, slammed the roan with forefeet. Even at this half-mile distance Tyree heard the drumbeat sound of impact, saw the roan stagger back. The bay went for the jugular again, the roan off-balance. The roan horse twisted, the bay slammed into him, and the roan went down on its flank in the shallows of the pool. It tried to stagger up as the bay whirled, used its hind legs. Again that drumbeat sound, and the roan rolled completely over, came to its feet in the water. Lathered, flanks heaving, it shook its head dazedly. Again the bay charged, straight into the pool. On its feet, tail hoisted, bleeding from a dozen wounds, the roan barely evaded that ferocious onrush. Water sprayed; then the roan was running. It had given up, and it splashed straight through the pool, the bay hard behind; stretched itself as it fled up the far wall of the valley. Screaming, the bay pursued until the roan vanished over the ridge crest. There the younger stallion halted, pawing earth, whickering in triumph, a magnificent silhouette against the sky. Then it turned, cantered back down the slope to the water hole. Without hesitation, it craned its neck, showed its teeth, then mounted a waiting mare and coupled.

Tyree lay absolutely still, the wind in his face. For a moment he had toyed with the idea of trying to creep down there, rope one of the wild ones—but now he knew that would be suicide. The bay, still full of fight, would rip him apart the moment it caught his scent. In its present mood, battle fever mixed with lust, it would attack, not flee from, any threat whatsoever, including an unarmed man on foot, and one chop of those great jaws, one slam of those flinty hooves, would write finish to the life of Shan Tyree.

So there was nothing he could do but lie there until the bay dropped to all fours again. The big horse shook itself, pawed and screamed in triumph and fulfillment. Stretching its neck full length, low, long, oddly snakelike, it bared its teeth, dodging, racing, nipping, hazing its newly acquired mares into a band, making sure each knew who the new boss was. When at last it had the herd formed to its satisfaction, an old mare in the lead, the stud bringing up the rear, the wild ones moved off down the valley, following the watercourse.

Tyree lay there for a long time, regretfully watching them go. If he could just have roped himself a young mare— It would have been a fight to break a wild one out here with no corral, snubbing post or saddle, and yet a horse would have been his only chance. But especially in his present condition he'd not dared get cross-wise of that young stud.

Anyhow, he'd found water. That was the main thing. With the mustangs out of sight now, Tyree arose, stumbled down the hill. At the pool, still roiled with mud and droppings, he threw himself face downward, drank—but with sense enough not to drink too much at first. He soused his head, laid his gear aside, rolled into the pool with all his clothes on, let it cool his skin, let the water soak in through his pores. Than he drank again. When, dripping, he stood erect, he felt new strength coursing through him. Waiting until the cold, spring-fed pool cleared, he filled his canteen. Now his optimism returned. After the stud calmed down, the herd would graze its way slowly back up to the high ground. If he could come up on it when the wind was right . . .

Even his feet were better for a long soaking in the cold water. Shouldering the coiled riata, picking up the Henry, he moved off down the stream, fed by the pool's overflow.

He traveled perhaps three hundred yards before he halted. Already his clothes were drying, but for some reason a chill walked down his spine that had nothing to do with that. His eyes narrowed as he turned to look behind him. He had the eerie sensation that he was being watched, even stalked, by someone or something.

Then he saw it, standing on the slope of the far wall of the valley, and his gut clenched within him. The roan stallion, defeated, bleeding from a dozen wounds, had reappeared. Ears pricked, head low, it was like a carved statue watching him.

Tyree matched it for immobility, heart hammering. He saw the arch of the crested neck, watched the ears slowly lay themselves back, heard the deep snort that carried in the silence of the afternoon. He saw the roan, his scent strong in its nostrils, paw the earth with a forefoot, and he swallowed hard. This stud would be in even a fouler mood than the victorious bay. Likely it would be ready to charge anything that moved; even now it was working up its courage for battle again. And while it had not been able to beat the bay, it could grind Shannon Tyree to a pulp.

And yet that was not the thought uppermost in his mind as he eased, very slowly, the coiled riata from his shoulder. Here was a horse. And while he could not go to it, maybe it would come to him.

A long moment passed. Then the roan broke its stillness, trotted down the slope, head low, nostrils flaring, the crest of its neck thick and swollen. Tyree waited, slowly paying out rope.

He watched the horse splash across the stream, halt again, now only a hundred yards away. Once more it sniffed the air, moved its head snakelike, pawed the ground. It could see him now as well as smell him. Then it went on with its demonstration.

Tail high, head low, it trotted around Tyree in a half circle, keeping that three hundred feet of distance, halted, pawed, half-circled again. Tyree, rope ready now, turned, following its every move. He was no longer thinking, feeling; all instinct, latent reaction, he never took his eyes from the roan.

Once, twice more, it made that half circle, edging closer every time, building up its courage and its fury. Then, with an explosive, deep-throated grunt, it charged.

Tyree moved quickly, shifting position, waiting until

the last minute. The roan was only forty feet away when the loop snaked out, low and open, seeming to stand on its end. A *mangana*, that throw was called, and Alvaro had taught it to him years before, forcing him to practice until he was wholly expert. He saw the stallion's bared teeth, foaming jaws, laid back ears, stepped sideways again, and jerked, using all his strength. The loop, like something with its own life, closed around the on-racing stud's forefeet, both of them, just above the pasterns.

Tyree leaned back against the rope with all his weight and power, digging in his bootheels. The stud hit rope's end with a force that almost jerked Shan off his feet. And when it did, with a sodden sound it crashed to earth.

Even as it hit, it let out a scream of rage. Immediately it tried to scramble up. Tyree ran for life, changing the direction of his pull. As the stallion managed to come up, he jerked again and once more it crashed over on its flank with jarring impact.

And now it was a duel, a test of strength, between man and horse, played out in the searing heat of midafternoon. Each time the stallion tried to rise, Tyree ran to get new leverage, and each time he threw it.

He had to, his life depended on it. Man and horse were linked inextricably now, and if he ever gave it slack enough to come up that sixty feet of rope after him he would not last a minute. It was, he thought blurrily, like having a bear by the tail; then he quit thinking altogether. There was only the nightmare now of saving his life, his own strength and quickness outlasting the roan stallion's.

If the big horse had been fresh, Tyree knew, he would never have had a chance. But its fight with the bay had used up most of its tremendous resources already. Hunger and exhaustion had claimed most of his as well, and like the stallion, he was panting, bathed in sweat. The world seemed to swim, his lungs gulped for air, there was nothing in the universe now but himself, the rope, the horse. . . .

Ten times, twelve, fifteen, he had no idea how many, he threw the stud. His ungloved hands were raw and bleeding, his legs and shoulders an agony of aching. But each time the big horse fell, it was slower trying to climb up. One more time he let it rise, even slacked the rope. Feeling that, it tried again to charge, and Tyree hobbled in a crippling run to change the angle of his pull and laid all his strength back against the braided rope. When the stud crashed down this time it was with an impact like that of a great tree falling. Flanks heaving, whole body white with lather, eyes rolled back and nostrils flaring, it raised its head and dropped it, making no effort this time to rise. Its exhaustion was complete.

And now Tyree knew, gasping for breath, he had his only chance. With the last of his strength, he took the final risk, rolling out the rope as he ran toward the stud. A hind foot flailed, and he got a turn around it, and then another, jerked hard and brought it up level with the forefeet. Wearily, the stud raised its head, tried to bite; Tyree heard the click of its teeth a foot away, as he took up slack, tied off. Then he had the horse hogtied and there was no way it could rise and menace him. With the sky seeming to reel overhead, he sank down on the ground, for the two minutes' rest he dared allow himself.

✖ Chapter 3 ✖

Once up, he worked quickly, deftly, knowing the roan would quickly regain its strength. His raw hands shook as, with the pocket knife, he cut the slack of the riata into sections. Tired as he was, it was as if *Tío* Alvaro was at his shoulder the whole time, guiding his every move.

First he got a small loop around the stud's jaws so he would not have to fear its teeth and tied that tightly. Then—there was no explaining it, but Alvaro had learned it from the Indians and swore it worked, and sometimes it did—he crouched before the stallion, blowing his own breath straight up its flaring nostrils. *That way he learns you,* Alvaro had told him. *Who and what you are. It is, maybe, a quick introduction. Anyhow, they say it lessens the fear a wild one has of man.*

After doing that, he want to the stream, filled his hat

with water, came back and poured it over the wild horse. He repeated that several times; otherwise, tied here in the awful sun, exhausted, it might well die on him. Then, before it had revived too much to fight its head, he fitted on the double-reined hackamore fashioned from the riata, with the noseband tight over the painfully sensitive nerves it was supposed to control. He improvised a breast strap and a short martingale so the horse could not throw its head. After which, with the remaining rope, he made the surcingle, pushing it beneath the fallen animal with a stick broken from the brush that grew along the stream. Tying it tightly, he built a handhold on it. There was enough riata left over to make stirrups, but he decided against that. If the horse threw him, he did not want a foot tangled in a rope contraption. Instead, he plaited three lengths together to make a heavy quirt. There was no time to treat a ten-year-old wild stallion like a colt fresh for the breaking; come tomorrow morning there would be another duel, one of pure brute strength, which he'd have to fight American bronc stomper style.

For now he'd done all that he could, and the sun was slanting low. He checked the hogtie knots; the horse, regaining strength, had begun to struggle. Once sure of them, he gathered brush from along the stream. Comanches or no, there'd have to be a fire tonight; otherwise the wolves that would catch the scent of the downed animal would eat it alive for all he could do—and maybe him as well.

He spent a chill night huddled against the stud's back, warmed by that and the fire in front of him. The wolves came, all right, and the coyotes, but the fire kept them off. Somehow Tyree, despite his exhaustion, forced himself to keep awake, keep feeding the fire on brush and buffalo chips. His own life and the horse's hung on that.

And, all through the night, he stroked the trembling, struggling stallion, scratched it between its ears, accustomed it to his feel and smell.

After forever, morning came. Hunger had gnawed at Tyree's belly through the night, but with the sun's rising the pangs vanished; he felt oddly clearheaded, light and agile, eager for the test to come. The empty rifle would have to be abandoned: this would be a two-handed job all the way.

The horse was strangely quiescent as he wrapped his bandanna around its eyes. Dehydrated by fighting and exertion, stiff from lying hogtied, as well as the aftermath of its battle with the bay and with himself, it would never be weaker than it was right now. And so it might as well be done and gotten over with. He took the empty revolver from its holster, stuck it in his belt, where he could get to it in a hurry. Then, positioning himself carefully, he cut the hogtie knot, after gathering up the reins of the hackamore.

Blindfolded, the stud hardly seemed to realize that its feet were free. Tyree had time to snatch a section of the rope, loop it in his belt; he would need it later. He held the reins tightly in his left hand. With his right, he leaned forward, jerked off the bandanna, then grabbed the hand-hold on the surcingle. "Now, you sonofagun," he yelled, "buck your heart out!"

The stallion blinked, tried its legs, and then, snorting, it was scrambling to its feet, and when it came up, Tyree was on its back.

For one long moment, it stood trembling. Then, suddenly aware of the weight on it, the stud snorted, grunted, and stiffly began to crowhop, back humping under Tyree's rump. Shan rode the first few jumps easily, pulling back on the reins. But he was not deceived. As soon as the stud had its circulation back—

It came with a rush, and all at once what was between Tyree's legs was a plunging, leaping fury. Straight up, the stud went, swapped ends, came down stifflegged, kicked and leaped and turned and plunged again. Earth and sky whirled crazily as Shannon Tyree clung grimly, riding for his life, on an animal that never before had felt the weight of man.

With all the muscle in his left arm, he did his best to keep the stallion's head up. The martingale, the muzzle, kept it from throwing it back too far or swinging it to bite him. Nevertheless, he took a terrible pounding. He could feel his guts being jarred within him each time the horse came down, and worst of all there was no pattern to its bucking, no rhythm that he could catch. It just fought madly to dislodge that creature on its back, and he fought back instinctively, saved only by his deathgrip on the surcingle's handhold.

A minute, two, three, maybe five they fought it out there in the valley. Blood trickled from Tyree's nostrils, his brain blurred, his spine seemed about to snap. Once the stallion reared, tried to throw itself over backwards. Tyree let go the surcingle, seized the pistol, and slugged the horse with all his strength between its ears. Dazed it came to earth again, and Tyree let the Remington go flying, fought for the surcingle handhold once more.

After that, slowly but surely, the stallion's fighting began to lose its edge. Not even such a mighty animal could keep bucking at that rate for long, and this one, weakened by thirst, hunger, the stiffness from yesterday, had to give out soon. But Tyree was weakening, too, dazed and pounded. Even though the fury of the bucking ebbed, he could barely sit the weaker jumps. If the horse found some new reserve of strength—

It did, for three jumps, four. Sunfishing, swapping ends, it put everything it had in those last few bucks. Then its fighting ebbed back into easier crowhopping, and just in time. Tyree's weary legs were losing grip, all sense of balance leaving him.

Suddenly the horse gave one last mighty lunge. Tyree felt himself going, forward and sideways simultaneously. He was half over the animal's neck when it came down, but his hand was still tightly locked in the surcingle. He caught a heel on the horse's shoulder, levered with a leg and with his right hand; then somehow he was in position behind its withers once again. Now blood ran from his mouth from bitten tongue and lips as well. But all at once it was over; trembling, white with lather, the roan gave a few more feeble jumps, then broke into a run.

Tyree let it stampede on down the valley, praying that it would not fall. It ran a mile, two, and then began to slow. Presently it came to a full stop, head down, flanks heaving, foam drooling from its muzzled jaws. And, for the moment, Shannon Tyree knew that he had won. He would have to watch it every minute—but he had a horse again.

Wearily, he let it breathe for a moment while the world came back into focus. Then he lashed it with the quirt. Instead of bucking, it responded with a snort, a stiff, bone-jarring trot. Tyree seized a rein in either hand, up short. Then, proving to the animal that it must follow the commands of those lengths of rope or have its nose hurt, he began to pull the exhausted animal in circles, teaching it to rein.

Two patient hours of that and he was at the outer limits of his strength, but now the horse vaguely understood, responded. What it craved now was water. Tyree reined it to the stream. It could suck up water through its teeth despite the rawhide muzzle. He let it drink sparingly, then succeeded in forcing it against its will from the stream. At his urging now, it walked, and when it had cooled down, he let it drink again. Then, feeling as if someone had worked him over with a sledgehammer, he pulled the horse eastward by main strength, and set out for the caprock, determined to get down off the Llano Estacado.

All day long they moved across the plains, and there was not a single instant of that journey in which Tyree dared relax his vigilance. Determined as he was to keep the horse too exhausted to fight any more, twice more it came apart without warning, and only his alertness saved him, that and the surcingle handhold. Yet each time he fought it, won, he knew that he was that much closer to proving his mastery of it, to having it at least semibroken. But by tomorrow, with no food in his gut for more than two days, would he still have strength left to handle it?

With still a few hours of summer daylight left, the character of the country began to change. Now, instead of that sealike rolling vastness, it was breaking up, into canyons, draws, and washes. He had finally made his circle back to the edge of the Llano Estacado, and now, he thought gratefully, the change in the monotony of the landscape reassuring, he had at least a fighting chance of reaching civilization.

Then, without warning, the roan halted, laid back its ears, pivoted on hind legs. Tyree grabbed the surcingle, yanked back on the reins. The stallion snorted, paying no attention to the pressures of the hackamore; suddenly, weak as it was, it bolted. Tyree swore as, with strength he never had suspected that it owned, it broke into a run, heading back the way they'd come. He laid back on the reins with all his muscle, fighting to regain control: he might as well have tried to stop a landslide. The big stud was stretched out in a dead run, and there was nothing Shan could do but hang and rattle. And all at once, even above the drumming of the stallion's hooves, he heard the thunder.

A low dull rumble, it came from westward; and Tyree's spine went cold, for mixed with it was a wild whooping, shouting. Comanches! he thought. Comanches, a lot of them, coming at a run, and this damned horse was carrying him straight toward them!

Then he saw them, flooding out across a rise, a tide of them all the colors of the rainbow, pounding toward him fast and hard—a great band of mustangs, a hundred, maybe more, wild horses. The stud had caught their scent, was stampeding to join them. But what made Tree's heart leap was the sight of riders flanking them—misty shapes lost in the cloud of dust raised by the herd. Indians or—? Then one emerged from the dust long enough for him to see briefly the outline of a sombrero, a coiled rope upraised, and relief surged through him in a wave. Whoever they were, they were not Comanches—then there was no time to think, only to ride, because Indians or not, he was in bad trouble. The runaway stud was going to crash straight into that wild bunch, and what happened then was going to be violent and dangerous.

On they came, the mustang band, and the stallion rapidly closed the gap between that tidal wave of horses. The old mares in the lead saw the approaching rider, tried to swerve and turn, but they were caught between the outriders herding them, and if they crashed into the stallion and it went down, that would be the end of Shan Tyree. He pulled hard at the reins, the stud ignored him, and then, at the last instant before a head-on collision with the herd, whirled, reared and pawed the air, came down hard and began running with them.

Suddenly Tyree was caught up in a sea of running mustangs. They closed around the stallion, and back with its own kind again, it raced with them. Bay, brown, chestnut, dun and pinto, they surged around Tyree and the roan, and the world was a blur of dust, of thundering hooves, and the rank odor of sweating horseflesh. Tyree prayed that the exhausted stallion could keep its feet. If it went down, he'd be minced in an instant beneath the hooves of the rest of the band.

On they swept, unchecked, uncheckable, across level ground, then down a slope. Vaguely, he was aware of the walls of a canyon mouth rising around them. A big mare slammed into the stud, almost knocked it off its feet; lurching, it regained its balance and raced on. Tyree, nearly thrown, managed to slip back behind its withers. Then, through the swirl of dust, he saw ahead how the canyon walls pinched in, and his raw hands redoubled their grip on reins and surcingle. When the herd poured through that notch, there would be crushing pressure—

It came, the wild ones sensing a trap, milling, trying to turn, heavy bodies slamming against Tyree's legs, the stud tossed among them like a chip on white water. Behind him he could hear men whooping, screaming, swearing. Then they had passed through the notch and were in the open again, and now the herd was spreading out, the pressure easing. The grass was heavy here on the canyon floor, some of the dust subsided. He saw sheer walls rising on every hand; some of the mustangs ran full into them, tried to paw their way up, fell back. Then the herd really began to mill, swirling, snorting, whinnying; a stallion screamed in fury somewhere behind. Tyree's stud was as wild as the others, every vestige of the slight training he had given it long gone. It ran wildly among the mares, and only the years of superb horsemanship behind him enabled him to stick on its naked, sweat-slickened back; to be dislodged would be to be knocked down and trampled in an instant. Nearly blinded by dust and sweat, he hung on grimly, and then he felt an arm encircling his body with an iron grasp.

"Up behind me—quick!" The voice roaring in his ear was hardly audible above the pounding of hooves, the screaming of the trapped wild ones. A big sorrel was crowding up beside the dun, and its rider pulled hard. Tyree's cramped hands came away from their holds; he grasped the man beside him, felt himself pulled loose, and then he was on a horse's rump behind the cantle of a saddle. He locked his arms around the rider, aware that the man had turned the sorrel somehow in all that confusion, was heading back toward the notch. With superb horsemanship, his rescuer fought through the plunging herd, using a coiled rope to lash his way, clear a path.

Then they were through the notch, out of the confusion and the danger, and as the rider checked the sorrel, Tyree was aware of other men quickly erecting a barrier of heavy poles in place across the narrowed space of the canyon.

"Pitt!" the rider roared. "Hold this hawse!" Then someone had the reins of the sorrel, itself excited by the proximity of the mustangs, and Tyree felt arms encircling him, felt himself pulled down. His feet hit solid ground for the first time in hours; his cramped legs sagged at once. The arms held him, lifted. "Awright," a voice said. "Awright, you're okay now." He looked up into a sweat-streaming face black as tar beneath its powdering of dust. And then Shan Tyree passed out.

Water in his throat, then the bite of whiskey, revived him. Opening his eyes, he found himself stretched full-length on the ground, surrounded by nearly a dozen dusty, chap-clad men staring down at him with intense curiosity. They were all white. The man kneeling beside him with the whiskey bottle, though, was black, a Negro.

"Now," he said. "Some more water." Tyree drank from the canteen, lowered it.

"Food," he gasped, astonished at the weakness of his own voice. "Ain't et in more than two days—"

"Supper in a while. Start with these." From a saddle bag, the black man took three cold biscuits, almost as hard as rock. Tyree seized and gnawed them eagerly. When they were gone, the black man gave him another drink of whiskey. The instant it took hold, along with the food, Shan felt strength returning. As he sat up, the black man said, "My name Whitton—Elias Whitton. This a crowd from Rancho Bravo. We out mustangin'. But we never allowed to round up you along with that wild bunch. That roan stud, he's pure wild all the way through. No saddle, no bridle, nothin' but that belly-band and hackamore. What the hell you doin' on him, how you come to be in such a fix?"

Tyree licked his lips. Trying his voice, he was surprised to find that it worked normally. His head, too, was wholly clear. That was good, because he had to select what he said very carefully. "Well," he said, "I'm from California, but I got the itchy foot and—" He went on to tell his story, including the *cibolero* camp, but omitting any mention of Velasco's stallion. He had fled up over the caprock, his mount had broken its leg, he had a duel with the stallion . . . He saw in the faces above him a growing incredulity.

"Wait a minute," one of the men cut in. He was tall, wideshouldered, with a barrel chest, lean hips and rider's legs. In his late thirties, his shag of hair, trimmed mustache, were threaded with gray, his face hard and rough-hewn, eyes a dark, cold blue and full of doubt. His Colt was worn high for riding, but tie-down thongs dangled from the holster, mark of a man who had probably been a gunfighter in his time. "You tryin' to tell us you roped and broke and rode that wild roan stud out yonder on the Llano without no help, no snubbin' post, no anything— Did all that and rode him thirty miles? You expect us to believe that?"

Something in his voice rasped Shan Tyree's nerves. "I don't give a damn what you believe. It's what I did."

"Hell, nobody could've—"

"Bancroft," the black man, Whitton, cut in quietly. *"I*

could've." He jerked his head. "Anyhow, yonder's the proof on the stud."

The man named Bancroft looked at Tyree for a long moment with eyes strangely hostile. "All the same, it's hard to swallow," he said and turned away.

Whitton's mouth twisted slightly in a grin. "I think Bancroft's a little jealous." Then he sobered. "Anyhow, that was some horse-handlin'. You a bronc stomper by trade?"

"I'm a horse-breaker by trade," Tyree said. "Yeah." He saw in Elias Whitton's eyes that the black immediately recognized the distinction he had made.

"Whichever you call it, there damned few men, white, red, or black, that coulda brought it off. Now, I got to put some medicine on them hands of yours. You look like somebody run you through a hammer-mill. Then we rope that stud, take off that tie you put around his mouth. He needs to eat. He a damn fine animal; you want to sell 'im, Rancho Bravo'll buy him from you. Just the kind of sire we lookin' for." Elias Whitton stood up, turned toward a wagon that had been brought into the canyon.

"Hold on a minute," Tyree called.

Whitton turned.

"Rancho Bravo. What the hell is Rancho Bravo?"

"Why," the black man answered, "it's a ranch. The biggest one west of the Pecos. It run from all the way up here clean down to the Santiagos, above the Big Bend of the Rio Bravo. Me, I'm a quarter owner of it. And I wouldn't be surprised if we had a place for a man like you. Now, you lay still while I git that medicine."

Tyree followed him with his eyes as he went on to the wagon. A nigger? he thought. A quarter owner of the biggest ranch in this end of Texas? Questions roiled in a mind too tired to deal with them, and he lay back on the blanket, not caring what Rancho Bravo was, so long as it gave him a chance to rest and fill his belly.

"Grease and pine pitch and some other stuff I learned from the Comanches," Elias Whitton said as he spread a black mixture over the rawness of Shannon Tyree's hands. "A medicine I learned. I lived among 'em, adopted into the tribe. Only I give it up after a while and went into the ranchin' business."

His touch was as gentle as a woman's. Reading the question in Tyree's eyes, he smiled. "Awright, yeah. I black, used to be a slave. Run away, out here to the big open, where the white men couldn't track me down. Comanches took me in because hawses my specialty, too, and they admire a man that really knows 'em."

He began to wrap Tyree's hands with bandages. "Then the War over and I free and I head back east, fall in with a man name of Henry Gannon. He a ex-Confed'rate, and he own a awful lot of longhorn cattle, but the Yankee occupation take his land for taxes. Me, I figure why not move all them cattle out here where they ain't no Yankee occupation and all the grass in the whole wide world? Gannon went for it, and a couple of other white gentlemen joined us. Loosh Calhoon, he was a captain in the Confed'rate cavalry, and Phil Killraine, he was a captain in the Union horse soldiers. The four of us, we form what we call Rancho Bravo."

He went on to tell how they had managed to shove four thousand cattle from the brush country south of the Nueces to the Pecos, overcoming every obstacle—long, dry drives; rustlers; Indians. "Split the herd at the Horse-head Crossin' and Gannon and Killraine took two thousand steers up to Pueblo, Colorado. Them miners up there starvin' for beef, and ours the first big herd to git there since before the War. Got top prices, used that to bring more herds west. Now we runnin' maybe fifteen thousand head. Sell 'em to the mines, the Army posts that have reopened out here, doin' well. There." He tied off the last bandages, and Tyree felt the medicine begin its soothing work.

"Anyhow," Whitton continued, "we all got our specialty. Henry Gannon, he's a master cowman, the cattle's his business. Phil Killraine can squeeze a two-bit piece until it bellers—he runs the finances. Loosh Calhoon, he about the best fightin' man there is—and we still got fightin' to do, against Mexican raiders, hawse thieves, and God knows what else. Me, I keep peace with the Comanches—this is their country, after all, and see that we got the remuda that we need. It take a lot of hawses to run an outfit like Rancho Bravo. That why we out mustangin'. This country crawlin' with wild hawses, and we need every mount we can git."

He stood up. "Matter of fact, we're settin' up a special horse ranchin' business. There a market for cavalry remounts, too, now, and some of these wild ones got good blood in 'em. Frank Bancroft yonder, the feller that couldn't believe you did what you did, he's gonna be in charge. First class hawseman. Only he work American style, you understand? Everybody got his own way of breakin' hawses. Me, I do it like the Comanches, slow and easy. You, I judge, handle 'em same way, the old *Californio*, Spanish way. Bancroft, he believes in doin' it his own way, and that a lot quicker than ours. Well, he gits good enough results, and we ain't got time to make every mount a top cuttin' horse. Anyhow, you interested in a job, I speak to him about you. We payin' thirty a month and found, and more if a man proves hisself a top hand."

Thirty a month! Tyree grinned. How Doc Meredith would jeer at that! But Doc had never been through what he had experienced in these past few days. "Elias," he said, "I would be interested."

"Hoped you would. Now, you get some rest and we'll see to that stud. Supper ready soon." And as Tyree lay back down, Whitton turned away. Tyree sighed, and then he was fast asleep.

※ Chapter 4 ※

Shannon Tyree threw his breakfast plate in the wreck pan on the wagon tailgate and, with stiff fingers, rolled a cigarette. His hard young body had sprung back quickly after food and a good night's rest, and Whitton's medicine had wrought a miracle on his hands. He sucked the smoke deep into his lungs and savored it; then turned as someone called his name. "Yeah?"

"Come here a minute," the man named Frank Bancroft said. "Elias and I wanta talk to you."

Tyree took the cigarette from his mouth. The harsh tone of command in the big man's voice rankled him, and he felt a flare of anger. It had, after all, been a long time since he had taken any man's orders. Then he relaxed, checking his temper. Taking orders was something he'd have to learn if he intended to live by honest work from here on out. "Sure." He walked over to the fire, where Bancroft and Whitton stood.

"I reckon you know I'm in charge of this mustangin' operation," Bancroft said. "Now, Elias says you want a job, but whether you get one or not depends on how I size you up." He raked his eyes up and down Tyree's lean form. "What you got to say for yourself?"

"Not a hell of a lot," Shan kept his voice easy. "Except I've never done anything in my whole life but work with horses. I figured the way I came in on that stud would say the rest."

"Well, it don't. It says you're good with a rope and that you can ride. And," Bancroft added, "that you're lucky. But it takes more than luck to work for me. We're startin' a new operation here, and before I git through, it's gonna be one hell of a big horse ranch. The man that works for me has got to take orders and do things my way. And my way ain't spendin' six months breakin' a colt, the way you *Californios* do. We got to turn out cow horses and we got to turn out remounts, and a lot of 'em, in a hurry. We're gonna go from can to can't, daybreak to dark, and there won't be any time-servin' and coffee-coolin' on the job."

Tyree looked at him. "You pay me wages, I'll guarantee to earn 'em." His voice was cool, and he could not help the insolence that tinged it. Bancroft seemed determined to rub him the wrong way.

"You damn well will." Bancroft glanced at the bandaged hands. "All right. It'll be a while before you can earn your salt ropin' or ridin'. But I reckon you can shoot. You'll start by killin' culls."

Tyree stiffened. "Wait a minute. You mean shootin' horses?"

"Ridin' that stud didn't ruin your ears, did it? That's exactly what I mean."

Instead of answering, Tyree turned to Whitton. The black man stood there, face impassive, and suddenly Tyree understood. Owner or not, there were damned few white men who would take orders from a black one. Whitton was in a strange and difficult position—theoretically the boss, yet needing a white mouthpiece, a white majordomo, to speak for him before anything could get done. "Well, I never counted on having to do that," Tyree said.

Before Bancroft could speak, Whitton cut in softly. "It ain't work anybody craves. But it got to be done. There good horses in that bunch, but there scrub mares and stallions, too, and they can't be left alive to breed, or eat the grass we'll need for other stock. And soon we'll be bringin' in top-grade stallions to breed up the herd, and some blood mares, too. Before we get through, we're goin' to try to clear this range of as many mustangs as we can, and what we leave has got to be top-line stock. So if Frank says that's what we got to do, that's the way it is."

"Christ," Tyree said. "There's room enough up there above the caprock for a million horses. Why not just cut 'em out and let 'em run?"

"Because that ain't the way I do things," Bancroft said. "There's a right way and a wrong way and I do 'em the right way. Now, you want a job or don't you?"

"I break stock, I don't kill it," Tyree said.

"You do if you work for me and I tell you to," Bancroft said and turned his back on Tyree and walked away.

Whitton took an empty pipe from his vest, chewed on it. "Yeah, I know how you feel." His voice was soft.

"And I won't blame you if you want to ride on. We'll swap you a mount, a saddle and bridle and some spurs, maybe a gun, for that roan and you can be on your way. It up to you." He paused. "You see, *somebody* got to manage the horse division. Me, I got my hands full with the Comanches right now. With the Army back out here, they're all stirred up. So I need somebody I can depend on, and Bancroft's the man."

Taking the pipe from his mouth, he looked down at it for a moment. "There's reasons. Some of 'em maybe you can understand, some of 'em maybe you can't. But Bancroft has worked with horses all his life, like you and me. Befo' the War, he was a breeder up in Kansas, supplyin' the emmygrants that traveled the Oregon and Santa Fe trails with stock. He got a reputation as a man that knows his stuff that's followed him all the way to Texas. And he's a worker, a driver, he gits things done—"

"And he was a free-soiler, too, I reckon," Tyree said pointedly.

Elias nodded. "Yeah, he was that. Which means he'll work with a black man the way none of these Texas wildcats will. You may not understand why, but that's important. Anyhow, what he says makes sense, no matter how much it goes against the grain. We can't leave the scrub stock to breed—they jest like rabbits and they'll ruin our whole plans. It was Frank's idea to shoot 'em, but I went along." Again he paused. "He's a little rough the way he puts things, and he can rub yo' hair the wrong way, but mostly he's fair and square, we wouldn't have no other kind. He do seem to be kind of pickin' on you, but ... he's got a wife and kid and this job means a lot to him.

He might be a tad jealous, maybe a little worried that a man that could do what you did with that wild stud might put him in the shade. Anyhow, it's up to you. Sign on or ride on; that's all I can say."

"I see." Tyree turned away.

"Except for this," Whitton added. "A man that sticks with Rancho Bravo and knows his work and does it good—well, he'll be fixed for life. We're big and rich and we're gonna git bigger and richer, and there'll be a lot of opportunities for all sorts of folks—if they can cut the mustard. You can take the short view and figure thirty ain't worth it and ride out—or you can take the long one and shoot for the moon and maybe manage a division someday, if you got the goods. Anyhow, while we got the stock penned here, we'll cull and break it to drive and finish off at the main ranch. Me, I got business elsewhere, and I got to pull out today. So it'll be between you and Bancroft when I leave. Y'all work it out to suit yourselves."

He strode off. Tyree watched him go, then ground out the cigarette underfoot. Black or not, Whitton had struck some chord deep within him. *I wouldn't really be workin' for Bancroft,* Tyree thought. *It would be for him. . . .* He sucked in a deep breath. Besides, there was really no way around it. Bancroft was right about the necessity of shooting scrubs if they were going to run a real horse ranch. He stood there only a second longer, and then he went to the big Kansan, who was giving orders to the men. When Bancroft had finished, he said: "All right. Sign me on. But you'll have to furnish the gun and ammo. I left mine up yonder on the Llano Estacado."

It was rotten, dirty work, but to give Bancroft credit, he saw to it that it was done as humanely as possible. Because this canyon would be used over and over in the future as a wild horse trap, it must not be contaminated with the blood-smell. One by one, the animals Bancroft indicated were roped by a team of experts, dragged fighting out of the box-canyon corral—stallions, mares, some with foals at their sides, colts and fillies—and well up a side-draw to where Shannon Tyree waited with a Henry rifle. Nearly twenty animals out of the herd of about a hundred: he shot each cleanly, accurately between the eyes. It was a full day's work, and when it was done he felt contaminated with a filth that it would take a long time to wash off, but, returning to the wagon, he was careful to show no emotion. There was plenty in him, though—especially a grim dislike of Bancroft for deliberately handing him this foul job. It was, he thought, a form of breaking him to Bancroft's ideas of discipline—and if Bancroft broke horses as he broke men, he would ruin some good animals before he was through.

Meanwhile, the rest of the crew had performed enormous labors. A gate had been built in the barricade; outside it, a fire kindled. One by one they had fought over thirty of the wild ones to the fire, thrown, hogtied them, then branded them with the Rancho Bravo iron, a big *RB* on the left hip. The men of the outfit sprawled exhausted around the fire; Bancroft had driven them like a demon. Only the Kansan seemed to have energy left in him, as if it welled from some deep source, inexhaustible, within him. "Tyree. I want to see you at the wagon." His voice was crisp.

Slowly Tyree arose, followed Bancroft to the tailgate where they were alone. "We still got business to take care of," the Kansan said. "I've signed you on. How're those rope burns? Think you can make a hand tomorrow?"

"Somebody got a spare pair of gloves, I can."

"I got spares." Bancroft pulled a pair of gauntlets from his belt, handed them to Shan. "Now, Whitton says we're to trade for that stud." He took a piece of paper from his pocket. "Here's a bill of sale; you're selling us the stud in return for a saddle, bridle, and that *grulla* over yonder in the rope corral. He's part of my string. We'll issue you a rifle and a shortgun until you can buy your own, and a rope." Holding out a pencil, he said, "Sign here."

Tyree looked at him. "Wait a minute. I don't know that *grulla*. I figured I'd get a choice of horses."

"Well, you don't. It's him or nothing."

"Then maybe I better take a look at him. I don't sign nothing in the dark."

Bancroft's mouth twisted in his square-hewn face. "I say he's a fair trade for the stud, countin' all else thrown in. Take it or leave it."

Tyree stared at him a moment, then turned away. Walking to the rope corral, he singled out at once the animal Bancroft meant. Though not crowbait by any means, it was inferior to most of the animals in the remuda. "Let me," Tyree said, "rope him out and try him."

"You don't need to. He's what you get. You'll be loaned other horses to make up a string, but as far as ownin', it's him or nothin'."

Tyree bit his lip. The fact was that, counting saddle and bridle, the trade was fair enough. Still, he did not like having the *grulla* rammed down his throat. But any bro-

ken horse was better than none, and at least with his own
he would be independent, able to ride out when he took a
notion. And he might, he told himself, take a notion
damned soon if he had to keep on working under Bancroft.

At last he shrugged. "Okay, if that's the way it is."
They went back to the wagon and Tyree signed papers,
one transferring the Rancho Bravo *grulla* to him, the
other making the roan stallion Rancho Bravo property.

Bancroft folded that last one, tucked it in his pocket.
"All right," he said. "Tomorrow, we'll rope out that roan
and shoot him."

There was a long moment in which Shan Tyree stared
blankly at the other man. Then he said harshly, "The hell
you will."

"The hell I won't. I been watchin' that bastard all
day, and he's nothin' but trouble, a fighter, mean as hell.
He's a stranger in that band and he can't get it through
his head that he ain't the boss. He'll kick or bite anything
that comes near him, and before he's through, he'll ruin
some good horses." Bancroft paused. "Anyhow, we'll be
bringin' in blooded stallions from Mexico and that roan
will eat 'em alive if we leave him free to do it."

Tyree shook his head. He had killed too many horses
today. Besides, he felt a certain attachment to the roan.
They had fought it out, he and the horse, fair and square,
and he had won, and it had saved his life. "That ain't
what Elias Whitton said. He said it was to run free, sire
more colts."

"Whitton didn't watch it the way I have today. It's outlaw, through and through, and it'll never be anything else

but outlaw. It gets culled tomorrow." Bancroft turned away, with blunt arrogance that was like a slap across the face.

Tyree's temper exploded then, nerves taut-stretched for too many days snapping. One stride and his hand dug into Bancroft's shoulder, yanked the big man around. "Gimme back that paper!"

Bancroft's blue eyes met his. "No. A deal's a deal. And take your hand off of me, mister." He knocked it away. "I've broken horses and I've broken men when I've had to. But you got crippled hands and you been through a lot and—"

"Don't you worry about my hands or what I been through. You've run a double cross on me and I want that bill of sale back. I'll not see that stud killed!"

"It can't be helped," Bancroft said. Tyree barely heard the words. Swearing, he reached for the paper sticking out of Bancroft's pocket, and that was when Bancroft hit him.

Ears ringing, then, he was lying on the grass behind the wagon, Bancroft over him, looking down. "Maybe you'll make a hand," Bancroft rasped. "But if I got to break you, by God, I will."

Shannon Tyree got slowly to his feet, rubbing his jaw. Then he took the gauntlets Bancroft had lent him from his belt. The other man watched as Tyree drew them on. "Now," Shan said quietly, "that takes care of my hands. Now we'll see who breaks who."

Bancroft stared at him a moment. "Well, I see I got to do it," he said and his eyes flared, and then his fists were up and he came at Tyree, and there was something of the enraged stallion in the manner of his charge.

A hot white flame seemed to sizzle in Tyree's brain. He

laughed, and with the hard knowledge gained in a dozen barroom brawls when he and Doc were on their sprees, met Bancroft's rush, which was all brute strength, no science. Ducking Bancroft's one-two, left-right, he dropped into a crouch, drove his own left out straight, and Bancroft ran into it. Tyree's fist caught him just above the belt buckle, and Bancroft's breath gasped out, and Tyree straightened, knocked Bancroft around with a shoulder, slammed home a right. It snapped Bancroft's head around, drove him up against a wagon wheel. Tyree came in like a panther, aiming a follow-up right straight at Bancroft's nose. Bancroft rolled his head and Tyree's blow missed and Bancroft's big fist slung sideways caught Tyree on the temple. Shan lurched two steps, dropped to a knee, and Bancroft came at him as he struggled up. Dazed, Shannon jerked in close, almost belly to belly with the other man, between his arms, felt Bancroft slug his kidneys, and his own hands came up and clamped across Bancroft's face, bending the man's head backwards. Suddenly Bancroft jumped back, giving them both fighting room, and now, panting, they came together once more, each man slugging, head down, fists driving, fighting as blindly as two bulls. Tyree took punishment and dealt it, and neither would yield, and the sodden sounds fists made on flesh were loud in the silence.

Frank Bancroft outweighed Tyree by thirty pounds, but he was also ten years older. A minute, two, of that brutal blow-trading, and Tyree was losing wind, but he knew suddenly, instinctively, that Bancroft's wind was going even faster; so were his legs. He felt Bancroft yielding just a little, felt his punches losing steam. Disregarding all the pain Bancroft dealt him, he called on last reserves of strength, drove Bancroft further back. Nobody in the on-looking crowd of Rancho Bravo riders made a sound; Bancroft was disliked, Tyree an outsider; their neutrality was complete.

Then, sheerly by accident, Tyree landed another belly blow. A left, it drove straight home to Bancroft's solar plexus. He felt Bancroft stagger, knew he had him now, raised his head to aim a final blow—and that was when Bancroft hit him between the eyes.

His head snapped back; the world turned a somersault. Dazed, he was suddenly on the ground, with the knowledge urgent in him that he must rise before Bancroft finished him. But his legs seemed not to work. He managed to struggle up only as far as his knees, and his arms seemed to weigh a ton as he tried to raise them. Then he realized that Bancroft was not coming at him. Gasping for breath, the foreman, too, was on one knee, head down, spittle drooling from his mouth. *Now*, Tyree thought, and did his best to push himself erect, but even as he slowly managed it, Bancroft, chest heaving, was try-ing to rise as well. Then from down-canyon came a yell: "Rider comin'!"

And now Bancroft and Tyree were up, but neither seemed to have the strength to move. Panting, they only stood there, hands dropped, staring at one another, wait-ing for strength to return. Tyree did not even hear the galloping horse, and if Bancroft did, he gave no sign, but suddenly it was there, between them, and Elias Whitton's voice rang out: "What the hell's goin' on here?" His sor-rel swung, curveting on a short rein. "Frank? Tyree? You two gone crazy?"

Tyree sought breath to answer. "The stud—" was all
he managed.

Whitton swung down, slapped the sorrel on the rump
and it cleared out. Standing there between them, he was
short, blocky, solid as a rock. "Which stud? What about
the stud?" Then he shook his head. "Never mind. You
keep yo' distance from one another. Git yo' breath back.
Then we settle this. And the first man that tries to go
against the other, I'll lay a gun barrel longside his head!"

Tyree dried his bruised face on his shirt tail, then awk-
wardly rolled a cigarette. Lighting it, he looked at Frank
Bancroft standing on the other side of the wagon tailgate.
Elias Whitton chewed his pipe for a moment. "Now," he
said, "I figure the two of you can talk. I ride out for a
little powwow with some Comanches that important to
the company, git it finished quicker than I thought, then
come back here to find you two goin' at it like a pair of
bulls. Now what is this? Frank, you talk first."

He listened intently as Bancroft had his say. Then he
turned to Tyree. "Now, your side."

"It's like he told you," Tyree said coldly. "Only that
stud ain't the outlaw he claims. It's just that he don't
know how to handle it. Anyhow, it saved my life and I
won't see no man shoot it."

Something that might have been a smile played around
Whitton's face. It vanished, though, as quickly as it had
come, as he nodded. "Well, there is right on both sides.
We can't have that roan tearin' up good hawses. On the
other hand, he maybe ain't as bad as he seems to you,
Frank. He been through a lot, too, and a hawse like a
man, he got nerves that can git all frazzled out. All the

same, Tyree, if you the hawseman you claim to be, you know you ain't ever goin' to train no ten-year-old wild stallion to amount to anything, and he might have gone sour after what he been through, maybe he has turned killer. I reckon each side can give a little bit. Tomorrow, we'll take him out, all right, but we won't shoot him— we'll cut him. Once he's gelded, he can go his own way. That'll take the fight out of him."

Bancroft shook his head. "He still won't make a saddle mount and when he's cut he's no good as a sire. He'll just eat grass that can go to better use."

"Well, there still grass enough. And he save a man's life, whether he want to or not. That man has got to feel somethin' for him. Tyree—what do you say?"

"I say that's fair enough," Shan answered.

"Frank, you accept it?"

"I work for you," Bancroft said. "If that's the way you want it."

"Then it's settled. Except for one thing, and that's whether Tyree stays on or not. Frank—?"

Bancroft rubbed his bruised face, stared at Shan. "He can stay as far as I'm concerned. But from now on he takes orders and keeps his mouth shut."

"Tyree? We can use you mighty bad, we need anybody knows how to break a hawse."

Tyree hesitated. His gorge rose at the thought of taking Bancroft's orders. But curiosity about this Rancho Bravo filled him—and besides, he'd not run from anybody. "I'll stay."

"Then it's settled. Tomorrow," Whitton said, "we'll finish up the brandin'. Then we'll start this bunch for the home ranch. The Comanch' are gonna be huntin' buffalo around here soon, and that'll put a stop to mustangin' for a while. Now, we got a long day ahead come mornin'. Let's all turn in and git some sleep."

※ Chapter 5 ※

It was a long slow journey south they made, breaking the horses to drive, the herd stallion and old mares sidelined with a length of rope from hind to forefoot, long enough to walk, too short to let them run. It was superb grassland through which they passed, dotted with longhorns bearing the RB brand. At noon on the fourth day, they entered the wide mouth of another canyon and for the first time Shannon Tyree saw the headquarters of Rancho Bravo, and although he had seen the great haciendas of California, some in existence for a hundred years, it was still a thing to take his breath away.

"There she is," Elias Whitton said proudly, reining in beside him, pointing. "We built all that in jest four years."

71

It was a massive thing they had accomplished, its heart a huge stone fortress of a building with a roof of green and living turf—a place almost impregnable, Tyree guessed, against attack of any kind. Surrounding it were several houses of stone or whitewashed adobe, small only in comparison, each with galleries on three sides to give shade at any time of day, most with flower beds in full bloom around them. Beyond, there were a pair of long, low bunkhouses, stables, sheds, and a vast complex of pole corrals. All this was set in a shady grove of cottonwoods, through which coiled a clear, cool stream. Nearly a small town in itself, with outlying gardens, chicken yards and pigpens, it was an oasis of safety, beauty, order in this wild and enormous land.

"The big building," Elias went on, "has got room for everybody on the place, case we have Injun trouble. We have got our own treaty with the Comanches, but with the Army back and puttin' pressure on 'em, they gettin' touchier and touchier. Anyhow, there is a spring of water inside it, and it our office and warehouse and fort. Them smaller houses is for the partners and the married foremen. We got five women on the place now, and some little kids; our wives see to it we live civilized. Someday we hope to have more layouts like this—maybe as far north as Colorado. Anywhere beef can grow and there a market for it, that where Rancho Bravo want to be. Same way with horses. That why I glad you stayed on, and why I say there enough opportunity for you, Bancroft, anybody that can cut it." There was barely suppressed eagerness in his voice. "Now, let's take this band of broomtails on down!"

Bancroft was already shouting orders. The weary herd nickered as it smelled water, willingly allowed itself to be shoved on into the canyon, and at the sound of its approach women appeared on the verandas of the houses, and men gathered to watch the mustangs being herded through a wide gate into a big corral which held as many more of their kind, in a turmoil of dust and whinnying and shouting. Then the bars were closed, and Elias put his horse up beside Tyree's. "Now we home! You come on and meet my partners!"

Tyree nodded. From the corner of his eye, as he swung his mount, he saw Frank Bancroft trot his horse to the smallest house of whitewashed adobe. "Lacey!" the big man yelled, swinging down, and a woman ran down the steps, into his arms. Tyree caught only a glimpse of blond hair glinting in the sun, a trim ankle as she lifted her skirts slightly to run to her husband. Then they were riding to where three men stood before the big stone fort. "A fine bunch, Elias!" yelled one with red hair and a homely freckled face. "Looks like you made a good haul!"

"Enough to keep Bancroft and his outfit busy for a while, Henry! Brought something else, too—a new man for the horse division." He dismounted and Tyree followed suit. "Shannon Tyree, meet Henry Gannon, the big boss of this shebang."

"Tyree." The redhead was in his middle thirties, with an easy grin, but there was authority in the set of his angular rawhide frame, and Tyree did not miss the two Colts he wore, low on his lips. "Glad to have you with us. Loosh—"

Lucius Calhoon was darker, younger, a little more dapper, and wearing only one gun on his left hip. But he too carried that authority in the movements of his tall body. It was his left hand he put out to Tyree; Calhoon's right wrist ended in a stump bound with leather. He had, Elias said, lost his right hand in the war, had trained himself to be as adept with his left at most things as most men and considerably better than the average. "One thing," Elias had told Tyree earlier, "God help the man that draws against him—or Henry Gannon either."

"Welcome to Rancho Bravo, Tyree." Calhoon's voice had a softer, more southern drawl than Gannon's, and Tyree remembered that Elias had said he was originally from South Carolina. "And this gentleman is Philip Killraine."

Killraine was shorter than the other two, quick, bouncy, in his movements, his face adorned with a cavalryman's mustache, and though he wore range clothes, his hat was that of a Union cavalry officer. His voice was clipped, brisk with a New England accent. "Mr. Tyree. A pleasure. Now, if you'll come inside, I'll get you on the master payroll." Then he turned, as Bancroft strode up. "Frank! A good haul! Congratulations. Come on in while I sign up Mr. Tyree here, and have a drink and give us a full report. We'll have to get these horses down on the books—"

The office inside the stone fort was large, and the partners gathered there. Gannon poured drinks all around, and, as he handed one to Tyree said, "Of course, this is only for special occasions. Otherwise, no whiskey on Rancho Bravo and no gamblin'. Those rules are hard and fast. We all have to live together here, a long way from any place to blow off steam, and booze and cards lead to ill-feelin'. So if you're a man that can't get along without his drink, maybe you'd feel more comfortable somewhere else."

"You feed and water me and that'll do," Tyree said, grinning. "I'm a lot of things, but one of 'em ain't a rummy."

"Fine. Where'd you fall in with Elias and the outfit?"

"Henry," Whitton said, "that a story the like of which you never heard before—and well worth tellin'." And briefly he recounted how Tyree had captured the stallion and then been caught up in the mustang run. "That why I hire him on the spot. Since then he prove that he jest as good as I think he is—only he works old-time Spanish style, not Texas brush-popper. Of course, the final decision was Frank's. I got to tell you, Frank brought off that mustang run slicker'n calf slobber. Never seen one go easier. Only we're finished mustangin' now until after the Comanch' have had their fall buffalo hunt."

Calhoon nodded. "That with what you already got ought to hold us for a while."

"Yes. Now, let's get down to business." Behind a desk, Killraine opened a ledger. "First you, Mr. Tyree. Full name, age, and next of kin, if you please . . ."

"Shannon Garrison Tyree, twenty-seven, no next of kin, except I guess some relatives back east I never met and don't know about. My daddy was from Kentucky, originally."

"Very well. If you'll sign here . . ."

When he had signed the payroll, Killraine blotted it, closed the ledger, opened another. "Now, Frank, the horses to be added to our tally . . ."

Tyree listened, checking closely, as Bancroft with unerring accuracy rattled off an inventory of the entire herd. It was the mark of the horseman that each animal had become an individual to him in the past few days: age, sex, color, characteristics—he tolled off all of them as Killraine made entries in the ledger. When he was through, Killraine said, "Fine. This will give us enough geldings to handle that thirty-head remount order we've got from Fort Davis. They're paying premium prices for six year olds rough broken."

Bancroft grinned. "I can stomp out thirty remounts in no time. I reckon you'll want the rest for ranch use. Circle horses and the like?"

"Some," Gannon said quickly. "But right now what we're really hurtin' for is good cuttin' horses. We haven't range-branded half the increase that's been dropped this year. We're goin' to be running three, four wagons on the fall cow hunt, and we're short of good cuttin' and ropin' horses in the strings. I'd like about a dozen ready within the next two months."

Bancroft bit his lip. "That's a tall order, Mr. Gannon. Two months is hardly time enough to make a cuttin' horse out of a range-raw mustang."

"I'd help," Elias said, "but I've done promised to go on the fall buffalo hunt with the Quahadi band. And the way things are with the tribe right now, it's more important for me and my woman Smoke Rising to be with them than it is to work the horses."

Bancroft shrugged. "Don't worry. I'll manage it somehow." He looked at Tyree. "Now that we've got an extra stomper, I'll put him on the remounts and take charge of the cuttin' horses myself. But in no more time than you're givin' me, they won't be by no means finished."

"Sho," Gannon said. "It takes a lot of work and experience to make a good cuttin' horse. Just pick the ones that look like they might have some cow sense and are quick on their feet and get 'em started so we can work this fall. It's up to you—that's what we hired you for. Tyree, if there's any gear you need, Captain Killraine will issue it and take it out of your pay in installments. . . ."

"Thanks," Shannon Tyree said. "I'll try to make a good hand." And he meant it. Somehow, he already felt at home here at Rancho Bravo, as if, for the first time in his life, he was where he belonged.

During the days that followed, that feeling deepened, intensified. The four partners of Rancho Bravo were good men to work for, tough, authoritative, yet wholly fair. And the presence of the women added an extra dimension to the atmosphere of the ranch, taking off the boar-hog roughness men developed living only in the company of other men. Calhoon had married Killraine's sister Evelyn; Gannon was married to a striking blond woman named Irene, who had previously been the wife of an Austrian officer involved in Maximilian's war with Juarez of Mexico and killed by Indians; Killraine's wife, Jenny, surprisingly enough, had been a dance hall girl, but she fitted in perfectly with the other two who had been born and bred ladies; Whitton was married to a fullblood Comanche woman, who moved out with him to join the tribe on its hunt. But it was Frank Bancroft's wife, Lacey, whom Tyree found himself following with his eyes whenever she was within his range of vision. How a man like Bancroft could have won such a woman was a puzzling thing to him.

At least a decade younger than her husband, she was not a beauty in the conventional way, and yet there was something about the set of her features, cleancut and angular, dominated by huge gray eyes with long lashes, that intrigued him. So did her body, what could be seen of it beneath the voluminous dress of the era—small breasts, slim waist, and, probably, long legs beneath those skirts that nearly dragged the ground. What he liked especially was the clean, graceful way she moved, like a fine young filly, and her ready smile and instinctive, easy gentleness with everyone she encountered. Sometimes, taking a break from the hard, dusty work in the corral, he watched her tending the flowers on the veranda of the little house or playing with the five-year-old boy, Frank Junior, and something would move within him that he did not like and tried to squelch, yet could not help. She was another man's wife, he told himself, and that was that. But if someday a horse kicked Bancroft's brains out . . .

This morning, three weeks after his arrival at Rancho Bravo he watched her finishing watering the geraniums on the gallery of the little house and was almost relieved when she went back inside. Maybe, he told himself, it was just as well he'd hardly passed a dozen words with her and better if it stayed that way. He had worries enough as it was, with Bancroft rawhiding him day in, day out . . .

Finishing his cigarette, he slid down off the corral fence, went back to where the big gelding snubbed to the post in the pen's center waited with laid back ears and trembling body. One of an earlier bunch of mustangs run in by Whitton and Bancroft, it had been cut after gaining its full growth, and like all such horses was a handful, with a stallion's power, and memory of a stallion's instinctive behavior. Yet it offered him no real challenge—not so long as all he had to do was follow Bancroft's prescription for rough breaking.

Which was primarily a matter of brute force. "We ain't got time to fool around with any fancy *Californio* stuff," Bancroft had told him harshly. "You forget your goddam hackamores. Sack 'em out, start 'em on a curb bit, and ride 'em 'til they know who's boss. It's up to the Army to do the rest."

"Sure. Only, you start 'em with a curb, you're gonna be sellin' the Army a bunch of hard-mouthed, cold-jawed hammerheads. A few extra days of rein work with a hackamore—"

"Goddammit, didn't you hear me? We ain't got a few extra days. You do it the way I say or you draw your time."

"Okay." Tyree's voice was thin. "You're the boss."

"And don't you ever forget it." Bancroft had turned away.

But Bancroft himself was busy all day long in another corral farther down the canyon with the cutting horses, and that gave Tyree a chance to fudge. Now, as he approached the horse, he wondered if Bancroft had broken the woman to marriage the way he broke horses to the saddle. Maybe that accounted for the quality of shyness, the kind of sadness, that he imagined he sometimes saw on her face in their brief encounters. Living with a man like the Kansan must be pure hell for any woman with real feelings— "But that ain't my business, is it, old son?" he said to the gelding. With it snubbed up short, he rubbed it between the ears, spoke soothingly to it, stroked its neck. The horse walled its eyes, but it did not kick or strike. He had taken extra time Bancroft would have begrudged letting it get acquainted with him, giving it a chance to understand that this strange creature on two legs was not its enemy. The less it felt it had to fight him, the less he would have to hurt—and toughen—its mouth with the steel bit. Meanwhile, he had given it a chance to become accustomed to the saddle's weight, and, while it was still unridden, had worked it on the reins to accustom it to their pressures. Now, though, he had done all he could in the limited time allowed him; it must now have its first riding, and, of course, it would buck.

Tyree blindfolded it, gathered up the reins, swung into the saddle. The horse humped its back and shivered. He loosed the snubbing rope and for a moment the bronc stood absolutely motionless. Then he jerked off the blindfold and it exploded.

Tyree rode it easily, as he had ridden hundreds, maybe thousands, of its kind in his time. As it jumped and sunfished and swapped ends, grunting the ancient refrain of horse to bronc stomper—*Gonna gitcha, gitcha, gitcha!*—he did not hesitate to grab the saddle horn, for this was no cowboy riding contest, and he used just enough force and not one bit more to prove to it his mastery. There was none of the savage spurring, heavy quirting, used to prove to a bronc that bucking hurt it more than its rider. Instead, he intended to substitute a few extra ridings, even if he had to work overtime, so that it would serve the man who straddled it out of confidence, not fear. And finally, when it had exhausted itself, he did touch it with the spurs, put it round and round the corral, using this opportunity to teach it responsiveness to the bit and reins. He felt a certain gratification that his stolen patience had paid off; it worked on the bridle better than he had expected.

"Shan!"

The voice called his name and he carefully swung the horse, to see Henry Gannon sitting on the corral's top rail. "Come over here. I want to talk to you."

Tyree forced the weary bronc to the rail, slipped down and tethered it. "Yes, sir, Mr. Gannon."

"Climb up and have a smoke."

Tyree climbed the fence to sit beside the redhead, accepting the makings Gannon passed him. Gannon was silent for a moment, looking at the lathered horse. "I been watchin' you," he said at last. "You work a little different from most bronc twisters."

"Just put in a little extra time, that's all. A few hours can make a big difference in the way a horse turns out."

"Yeah. You remind me of Whitton. That's the way he works." Gannon paused, as if seeking exactly the right words for a delicate subject. "I been watchin' Bancroft, too, handlin' those cuttin' horses we need. Ordinarily this is a decision I'd leave to Elias but he ain't here. How would you like to take over the makin' of those cuttin' horses?"

Tyree's heart leaped, but he kept a poker face. "I'll do whatever you or Bancroft tells me to. It's all the same to me."

Gannon hesitated. "I got an idea you could do a better job on 'em than Frank. Now don't mistake me. Far as I'm concerned, he's still top man in the horse division. But everybody's got a little different touch with things. They don't come any better than Frank at grindin' out cavalry remounts or circle horses in a hurry, but he's havin' trou-

ble with those cuttin' horses. Or maybe I'm just too per-
snickety. Anyhow, they ain't turnin' out exactly to suit
me, and I thought I might give you a try at 'em if you
wanted it."

Now it was Tyree's turn to wait before he spoke. "To
be honest, Mr. Gannon, the only way I can make a cuttin'
horse is if I got a free hand to use my own methods. I
wouldn't want to try it any other way. And I got an idea
Frank Bancroft wouldn't be too happy about that."

"You leave that to me," Gannon said. "Now, you finish
your day's work here, and report to me tomorrow mornin'.
Okay?"

"Yes, *sir!*"

"Good." Gannon climbed down off the rail, walked
away. Tyree watched him go with a surge of triumph.
Score one for me, Bancroft! he thought, and unlatched
the horse's reins and without even blindfolding it swung
up into the saddle.

This time it hardly bucked at all.

It was work he loved, and he could hardly wait to get
to it in the morning, was reluctant to break off at quitting
time. Sometimes after supper he went back to the corral
to work with the dozen geldings. Time was short before
the fall roundup, and there was damage Bancroft had
done which he must remedy. Best of all, for the time this
lasted, he was out from under Bancroft's domination, his
own master once again.

What Gannon had said to the Kansan remained a mys-
tery to him, but it had been a rough pill for Bancroft to
swallow and it was still stuck in his craw, and that made
Tyree all the more determined to produce top mounts for

Gannon. Just the expression on Bancroft's face nowadays, the look in his blue eyes when they met was to Shannon Tyree like a slug of good strong whiskey. Bancroft was scared, and it showed—afraid that Tyree was a serious rival for the job of manager of the horse division.

And he was. For the first time in his life, Shannon Tyree was looking farther ahead than tomorrow's sunrise. He knew Rancho Bravo now, knew what a mighty thing it was, the enomous potential in its future, and there was a wanting like an ache to be a part of that future, an important one. Ambition was something new to him, but the resolve grew in him—he would wipe Bancroft's nose when it came to horses every chance he got, and he knew his efforts would not be overlooked by the owners. Give him three months, six, and with any kind of luck Bancroft would be working for him instead of the other way around.

With, it almost seemed, *Tio* Alvaro standing by his side, whispering advice in his ear, lending a hand when needed, he managed with superhuman effort to have the twelve geldings ready for the fall roundup. When, one by one, Gannon himself tried them on stock, the expression on his face was Tyree's reward for all his efforts. Sparing with his praise, Gannon nevertheless could not help bursting out one day, "I'll be John Browned, Shan! Those horses work like they'd been on the job a year! I never seen the like of it."

Tyree was careful not to look at Bancroft, who sat his own mount within hearing. "It's just the little extra time a man takes, Mr. Gannon."

"It's more than that," Gannon said. "I want six more

geldings broken just that way. You can do it while Frank delivers the remounts to Fort Davis."

Bancroft's voice cut in. "I'd aimed to take Tyree with me to deliver 'em, Mr. Gannon."

"I think you'd better pick somebody else. Anybody can drive broke horses. We'll let Tyree make us some more cutters."

"As you please," Bancroft answered, and almost sarcastically he touched his hat brim, turned his horse, and drummed off at a gallop toward the home ranch.

❊ Chapter 6 ❊

Simultaneously the roundup wagons moved out and Bancroft with five heavily armed men headed west with the cavalry remounts for Fort Davis. Only Calhoon and a corporal's guard were left behind to defend the home ranch and its women. Tyree was among them, and to him it seemed that with Bancroft's departure a great weight had lifted from his shoulders. For the two weeks the man was gone, he would have a completely free hand with the unbroken stock.

He was not the only one who seemed to feel that sense of freedom. On the morning after Bancroft left, he was carefully fitting a hackamore to the head of a snubbed four-year-old when he felt someone watching him and turned. There, looking through the rails, was Bancroft's blond wife Lacey, holding the hand of her son. Instantly Tyree took off his hat. "Mrs. Bancroft. Mornin'."

"Good morning, Mr. Tyree. I hope you don't mind us watching for a while." She smiled—the first time he could remember seeing her do that. "Frank Junior's like his daddy—just can't stay away from horses. And now that Big Frank's gone, he begged me until I brought him to watch you work."

Tyree walked to the fence, pulses hammering. It was strange, he thought, how one special woman could start that excitement in a man. It had nothing to do with beauty—although Lacey Bancroft was a pretty woman— nor anything else tangible he could put a name to. In his time he'd known many girls lovelier than she, but none of them had stirred that aching longing, that need for possession, that moved in him at the very sight of her.

"Why, I'd be mighty glad to have you watch. Not going to be much of a show this morning, though." They looked at one another through the rails. God, those huge gray eyes of hers—he felt an eerie dizziness, as if he'd had too much sun. "I'm just starting to hackamore break this horse. And the headstall has to fit just right for every animal. Some horses, they're what you might call light-headed and others heavy-headed. Wrong fit and the hackamore hurts too much—or not enough."

"Is that very important?"

"Well, a horse don't know what's goin' on when you start to break him. The gentler you can be with him, the quicker you win his confidence, the less he fights you."

Her eyes played curiously over his face for a moment. "Frank says it's the other way around. The important thing's to teach them who's boss right away."

"Well, everybody's got his own way of doing things."

"And yours," she said quietly, "seems to be very different from his. Well, please go on with your work, and we'll just watch a while."

"Yes, ma'am. Here, young feller. Climb up where you can see better." He helped the boy, owl-eyed and silent, up to the top rail. It would not have been ladylike for his mother to join him and she did not.

They stayed there until he was through with that colt, let him out of the breaking corral into the main one. By then it was midmorning. As he put up the poles, Lacey, who had taken the boy down off the fence, said, close behind him, "Aren't you about ready for a cup of coffee?"

Tyree turned, to look down at her now with no bars between them. For a moment, her eyes met his, then slid away. "That would be real nice," he said.

"If you'll come on over to the house, it wouldn't take long to make a fresh pot."

Tyree grinned. "That ought to be a lot better than the tar they keep on the cookhouse stove."

The little three room adobe house was neat as a pin, the flowers around it showing the results of loving care. In the kitchen, Tyree sat at the table while Lacey made the coffee and the boy played in the back yard. Just watching her movements made something ache within him, and he had to think hard to find conversation to break the silence.

"I understand you and Frank are from Kansas," he said at last.

"Yes." Her back was to him as she filled the pot. "But ... our luck ran out there and we decided to head west.

Texas seemed a good idea, and in San Antonio Frank met Henry Gannon and . . . here we are."

She fed wood into the stove, set the pot atop it. "And lucky to be here," she went on. "I was a little afraid at first . . . coming all this way out here. But Rancho Bravo's a good place to be. There are other women, and Frank has such a good job— You'll want some milk and sugar. . . ."

It was odd, Tyree thought later as she refilled his cup, how natural it seemed to be sitting here with her; the talk was no longer halting, awkward. He had told her about his childhood, about *Tio* Alvaro; what he did not mention was Doc Meredith or his days as a horse thief. That seemed a hundred years ago. And she, sitting across the table from him, sketched in her own background.

Her parents had been homesteaders in Kansas—until the terrible guerrilla battling in the state's eastern half during the War had wiped them out. "They weren't even soldiers," she said, staring down into her cup. "They were just bandits who called themselves soldiers. They just rode up and shot down Daddy and Mother grabbed a gun and they shot her, too. . . . Then they stole everything we had, burned every building on the place. If I hadn't been away that day, I guess they would have killed me, too. . . ."

"You shouldn't talk about it," Tyree said. "You shouldn't even remember it."

"There's not a day of my life I don't remember it. Anyhow, I was alone and broke and didn't know what to do . . . and then Frank came along. We each needed somebody and— It hasn't been an easy life, but we're making progress. And if everything works out here, at least Frank Junior can grow up with some security, and— We'll see to it that he has the kind of life we never did." Then, to his surprise, she laughed. "I'm sorry. I didn't invite you over to depress you with my tales of woe. More coffee—?"

He almost said yes. But now there was a kind of fear in him, a fear of what would happen if he stayed here too long alone with her. It might even be something she wanted to happen— But she was another man's wife and he forced himself to remember that. "Thanks, but I'd better get on back to work."

"Yes, I suppose so. Well, I hope you don't mind if we come and watch sometimes. And if you want a cup of coffee, anytime—"

"That's mighty nice of you, Mrs. Bancroft."

"Not at all, Mr. Tyree." They both stood up, and for a moment their eyes met. And Tyree could feel it, the thing that arced between them, a force as strong as lightning. Wordlessly, feeling both guilt and elation, he turned away and left the house. Striding back to the corrals, his brain raced like a wild horse in its first pen, thoughts circling, dodging . . . So—it had not been love that had brought her and Bancroft together. At least not on her part. She had simply needed a strong man to take care of her, had accepted the first to come along, out of desperation. Suddenly it seemed to him that Bancroft had everything he himself wanted, everything he would ever need to make him happy. The job, the woman— At first he had thought only about the job. Now he could not help wanting to rob Frank Bancroft of both.

* * * *

For the next four days she was at the corrals with the boy every morning; and the ten o'clock coffee became routine. The others on the place were bound to notice, men and women both, yet it was as if neither cared, could help it. Not once did he lay a finger on her, or she on him, and yet each time that electricity between them grew more potent. Sooner or later, Tyree knew with hope and dread, something was bound to happen—

Then one morning they were not there at the regular time. It was too bad, Tyree thought; he was topping off a horse that bucked spectacularly. He had saved the animal to put on a real show to impress both her and Frank Junior. But when they did not come, he told himself that maybe it was just as well. Nevertheless, he used quirt and spurs with unwonted fury as the animal unwound itself. By the time he'd finally ridden it to a frazzle, his head was ringing, his whole body ached. At first he hardly heard her voice, calling desperately. "Mr. Tyree! Mr. Tyree!"

He slid down off the bronc, snubbed the mecate instinctively, and turned. She was at the fence, face pale, eyes wide with fear. "It's Frank Junior! I can't find him anywhere! Have you seen him?"

Tyree's head cleared instantly, and he was over the rails in a pair of seconds. "Not hide or hair—"

"Oh, heavens, I hoped he was here watching you. He was playing in the yard and then— When I looked for him, he was gone!"

"Okay, calm down, he's somewhere around. We'll get some people and—"

Her scream sliced through his words. "Oh, no, oh, God—look!"

Tyree whirled, but she was already running. He stood frozen for an instant, then saw it, too—the tiny figure, trailing a length of rope, just dodging under the rails of the pen a quarter of a mile away in which there were twenty head of longhorn cattle.

Steers and cows with calves, they were the stock on which he trained his cutting horses, and this was a fresh batch just driven in off the range yesterday. Used to running wild and free, they were as fast as deer, as fierce as grizzlies—and only a man on horseback could dominate them. Without hesitation, they would charge a human on foot, especially the cows with calves, and now Frank Junior was in the big pen with them.

No man went unarmed on Rancho Bravo at any time; Tyree's gunbelt was on a fence post. Screaming her son's name, Lacey was far ahead of him; in a few long strides, legs pumping, he overtook and passed her, the Colt he'd snatched from holster in his hand.

That was the longest four hundred yards he'd ever run. Time seemed to stand still as the little boy straightened up, swung the short rope with the tiny loop in one end, just as he'd seen his father and Tyree do from horseback so many times. The cattle, all colors of the rainbow, long horns glinting in the sun, at first backed away, curious and a little shy of that strange figure. Panting, Tyree was within a hundred yards of the corral as the boy walked toward them. "Frank, come back!" he bellowed, but the child seemed not to hear, only approached the bunch of wary cattle steadily, wholly unafraid. Then one old spotted cow emerged from the bunch. She raised her head, sniffed, then dropped it, shook her horns, and a bellow that was a war cry split the air. Advancing a few steps, the rest following her, she pawed the ground, flinging dirt up over her shoulders with great, splayed hooves. Suddenly Frank Junior seemed to realize his danger. He turned and ran on stubby legs.

It was the worst thing he could have done; the old cow charged.

She was almost on him when Tyree, twenty yards from the pen still, fifty from the target, fired, on the run. It was a shot of desperation, and that it went home was sheer luck—or maybe a granted miracle. The slug caught the charging cow in the chest; she fell to her knees, and instantly the scent of blood drove the other cattle mad.

Now it was not the boy but the wounded cow that drew them. Longhorns were like that once they caught the scent of their own kind's blood. Frank Junior fell, scrambled up, as the herd charged the fallen cow. All at once the morning was hideous with a strange, eerie squalling scream and bellow, as the longhorns gathered around the wounded cow, pawing at her, goring her. But that respite, Tyree knew, would only last an instant. With that blood-madness on them, they would be doubly, blindly ferocious. Even now a steer turned away from the fallen cow, bawled, and raced after the stumbling child.

Tyree, dodging between the rails, fired again, at closer range this time, and the steer went down. Then he was in the pen, racing across it to scoop up the crying child. But now another cow, horns tipped with blood, broke loose from the knot of crazed executioners, lowered her head, came after Tyree. He fired another round, saw her go down, and then he was running for the fence. Behind him there was a rumbling of hooves as other longhorns charged.

He did not look back; legs pumping, he dove for the fence. "Here!" he yelled and literally threw Frank Junior between the rails straight into his mother's arms. Catching the boy, she staggered back, as Tyree dived through the fence, just ahead of lancing horns. He hit the ground hard, rolled, lay there panting for a moment, then scrambled up. The whole corral shook as a pair of heavy steers slammed into it. Threatening, pawing, they bawled that eerie blood-call of theirs, then turned to race back to attack with maddened ruthlessness the second fallen cow.

"Oh, Frank, Frank—" The woman hugged the child to her breast, tears running down her face. Then she lowered him to the ground, and Tyree caught her just as her legs gave way.

"All right," he said and he held her tight against him. "It's all right now—" He felt her breasts move against his chest, her hand close around his arm. Slowly she raised her face.

"Shan—" she whispered. "Oh, Shan—"

He would have kissed her then and there, but men were running toward the pen, drawn by the uproar, so he only held her and she leaned hard against him for a moment. Then she let him go, seized her son. "Oh, you— I ought to whip you so hard—" Instead, she held him closely to her, kissing his tear-wet face.

"Tyree," Calhoon began, coming up. Then he comprehended. "The boy—in there?"

"Thought he was gonna be a roper like his daddy. I'm sorry I had to kill those beeves—"

"The devil with the beeves as long as the boy is safe! Mrs. Bancroft, you'll have to watch him more closely!

Now, I think you'd better take him home, put him to bed or something." .

"Yes, sir." She took a few unsteady steps, still holding the child.

"Here." Tyree took him from her. "I'll tote him for you."

"Do that," Calhoon said. "The rest of you men— mount up and break up that cow funeral before those fool longhorns kill each other off. . . ."

Quietly she closed the bedroom door behind her, came into the kitchen. She had, Tyree saw, washed the dust off her face, combed her hair. "I told him," she said a little bitterly, "that if he got off that bed, I'd tan his hide." Her face softened as she looked at him. "I don't know how to thank you."

Tyree did not answer. Silence hung between them as their eyes met. He could still feel the places on his body where hers had pressed. Then, almost like people in a dream, they were moving toward one another and then she was in his arms and his mouth came down on hers. Beneath his lips, hers parted slightly; she strained against him; he felt her nails digging into the nape of his neck.

He had no idea how long the kiss lasted; it was an eternity and yet all too short a time before, suddenly, she pulled away, pushing his hands from around her waist. "No," she whispered. "No. This is wrong."

"It's right," Tyree said thickly. "Lacey, I know it's right. I've been wanting to—"

"Yes. So have I. Ever since you came." She turned away. "I don't know why. Maybe because you're so different from Frank. He can be so hard, so cold. . . . All the same, he is my husband."

"But you don't love him."

She would not look at him. "He's been . . . kind to me, as best he knows how. He's a good man. In his own way."

"All the same . . . Lacey, I love you. And you can't throw the rest of your life away—"

"Please." She rubbed her face. "Shan, go now. Go and let me think—"

He hesitated, standing there for a moment. "All right," he said at last and he went out.

Somehow he got through the day, but all he could think of while working with the horses was Lacey Bancroft. That night, in the nearly empty bunkhouse, the memory of her in his arms was still a torment that kept him staring at the ceiling long after all the other men were snoring soundly. Presently he could stand it no longer. Noiselessly, he swung out of the bunk, dressed, went outside.

Past midnight, Rancho Bravo lay sleeping beneath a crescent moon, though there were guards at the head of the canyon. Tyree walked beneath the cottonwoods, unable to cope with all the things roiling in him. Deep in shadow, he halted, rolled a cigarette, struck a match.

"Shan—" The soft voice made him turn. There was no mistaking the silhouetted figure that crossed from moonlight into darkness. Then he was holding her. "I couldn't sleep either," she whispered. "But I didn't expect—"

"Hush." His mouth silenced hers.

A long time later, when she took her lips from his, she

murmured, head pressed against his shoulder, "Oh, Shan, what are we going to do?"

"I don't know," he said, holding her tightly. "I just don't know. Take what we can get, I reckon."

They did, but it was not much, not nearly enough for Tyree during the next six days. There were eyes everywhere, and yet somehow they managed to steal moments—all too few—together at random times. There was a point beyond which she would not let him go, and beyond which he did not want to go, because he loved her and that was something that had to wait until somehow he had the right to do it. For the time being, their arms around each other, their mouths meeting, had to suffice.

And then even that ended. For Frank Bancroft returned from Fort David two days early with the government voucher for the remounts, all safely delivered. And once again Lacey—it seemed to Shan Tyree—was his prisoner.

On the day that Bancroft rode in, Tyree, in the corral, saw him come and felt a lance of hatred unlike anything he had ever known go through him. He saw Bancroft dismount before his house, embrace Lacey, kiss her briefly, hug his son, then go to report to Calhoon. His thoughts were dark and bitter for the half hour Bancroft was inside the fort and office building. Then the man emerged, saw Tyree working the gelding in the corral, and strode straight toward him, face set and grim.

Tyree's mouth went dry; his heart hammered with sudden fear. Edging the horse to the corral post where his six-gun hung, he stepped out of the stirrups, went down the outside of the fence. Bancroft came on steadily, spurs jingling, thumbs hooked in gunbelt, and now Tyree was certain. *He knows*, he thought.

"Tyree." Bancroft halted a few feet away.

"Yeah." To his surprise, his voice was steady.

"I heard about what went on while I was gone." Bancroft's voice was harsh.

Tyree sucked in breath. "Did you now?"

"Yeah." Bancroft's face seemed to spasm as if forcing out the words cost him pain. "And I owe you thanks. Lacey and Calhoon says those cow-brutes would have killed my boy for certain if it hadn't been for you. I am . . . obliged." And suddenly he thrust his right hand out.

Knees going weak, Tyree hesitated, took it. "Hell, anybody would have done it."

"Well, it wasn't anybody. It was you. So thanks until you're better paid." After which, with the air of a man relieved to get an unpleasant duty over with, Bancroft turned away and went toward the little house where his wife was waiting for him. For the first time in his life, Tyree felt an impulse to shoot a man in the back. Instead, he spat, climbed into the corral, and mounted the horse again.

✖ Chapter 7 ✖

The Chihuahua *rancho* was tremendous, sprawling across
the Mexican uplands, the *hacienda* that was its headquarters a great walled fortress, containing a luxurious main
house and a whole village of *vaqueros* and other workers
within its walls. Calhoon had ridden down from Rancho
Bravo first to negotiate the deal for the two fine Spanish
stallions and the twenty broodmares that would upgrade
the Texas horse herd. By prearrangement, Bancroft,
Tyree, and six Rancho Bravo men had followed a week
later. Now, as customary on Sunday mornings, in an
arena especially built for it, Don Diego Estrado Soto y
Gama, his sons and relatives, were practicing the arts of
the charro, the Mexican gentleman horseman and cowman. Today, sitting on the rough seats built for specta-

tors, they were laying it on a little thick, Shannon Tyree thought, to impress the *gringos*.

And were succeeding, he thought wryly. Calhoon, Bancroft, and the others were goggle-eyed at the caliber of horsemanship displayed by the Estrados. They had already witnessed the *cala de caballo*: the charros, beginning at the *lienzo*, the corridor leading into the arena, raced their horses at a dead run for three or four hundred yards straight toward the onlookers, then stopped them on a dime, reined them right and left, and finally backed them in a dead-straight line the full distance they had come.

All this was done with seemingly featherlike pressure on the reins and Calhoon swore in admiration. "How the hell do they train them like that?" He shook his head. "And using spade bits, too; I thought they were supposed to tear a horse's mouth to hell."

Tyree grinned. "In an ordinary cowboy's hands they would." He glanced sideways at Bancroft. "But that's really the whole idea behind the spade bits. Those horses are broken with mouths as tender as a baby's bottom. Then they respond to damn near no pressure on the bit. To a well-broken charro horse, the bit's nothing but a signal. . . ."

After that, there had been the *pialadores en el lienzo*, the roping of wild mares. With eighty-foot maguey riatas, the charros had caught the hind feet of the mares and then, instead of throwing them, as would American ropers, had slowed them gradually to a halt, still on their feet, paying out their long lines with a special technique.

Beside Calhoon, Don Diego was glowing with pride. Clad in the traditional charro costume—white shirt, leather chaps, enormous sombrero, spurs worn low on the heels, and, of course, pistol and cartridge belt—he was a man in his midsixties. He nudged Calhoon. "You see, we have our own way of doing things. I think you have no man among your people who know our style." His grin broadened. "Now they begin the *colas*. This time they will use no ropes at all. It is an art that originated in the state of *Jalisco,* but we have adopted it. The rider throws a wild bull—not with the *soga,* the long rope, but by his tail."

"I've heard of that," Calhoon said. "But I've never seen it. Bancroft—"

"No," said the Kansan tersely.

Then it was as if *Tio* Alvaro spoke in Tyree's ear or through his mouth. "I can do it," Tyree heard himself say.

Don Diego looked at him, dark eyes widening, smile turning to a kind of smirk. "Really?"

"With a horse that knows his business and a saddle built to take it."

"Neither would be any problem if you would like to try your luck. But it is not something I have ever seen a *norteamericano* rider do."

"I haven't tried it in years, but I learned it in California."

"Then if you wish—"

"Tyree," Bancroft broke in, "don't make us look like a bunch of damned fools—"

"Hold on," Calhoon said. "Shan, you really want a chance at it?"

Tyree hesitated. It called for split-second timing, and he would be on a strange horse and for an instant he wished he hadn't spoken. Then he looked at Bancroft and thought: *Another way to wipe his nose . . .*

"If you would be kind enough to lend me the proper horse and saddle . . ."

"It shall be done." The Spaniard snapped orders. Tyree followed Don Diego's majordomo. "Perhaps, Senor Calhoon," he heard the Spaniard say as he climbed down off the seats, "you would like to lay a slight wager—"

The minute his hands touched the reins, the horse knew that the man on its back had precise mastery of it. A fine bay, it trembled with excitement, eagerness, at the end of the corridor. Then, from a pen, the *vaqueros* hazed out the bull.

A huge animal, black as the ace, it shook its horns, raced down the corridor toward the *ruedo,* the arena, while the *vaqueros* shouted. Tyree slacked rein pressure, let the horse have its head. It was off like an arrow, in a few strides overtook the running bull. Tyree leaned from the saddle, slapped the bull hard on the rump with his right hand. Instantly its already uplifted tail raised even higher. With *Tio* Alvaro seemingly guiding his every move, Tyree seized the tail, kicked out his right leg, wrapped the tail around leg and stirrup leather both. At the same instant he reined the running horse sharply to the left.

The impact on both animals and on the man was terrific. One instant more and the bull would have dragged the horse down with it, but with precise timing, Tyree released the tail. A shout went up from the Spaniards and the Mexicans, and Tyree checked the mount on its haunches, spun it, just in time to see the bull go head over heels, land dazed. After an instant, it scrambled up, shook its horns, trotted around the ring. Tyree unlatched the saddle rope, worked out a loop. As a charro rode into the arena, he heel-roped the bull precisely. Again the animal ran, and Tyree paid out the high-raised rope, leaving the animal on its feet. As, slowing, it turned to charge, the other rider roped its head. Together, they worked it back to the pen, Tyree full of a wild exultation that was better than any drink, even though his hands sweated on the reins and rope. Then, touching the fine mount with spurs, he raced it into the ring, brought it to a skidding halt, swept off his hat and bowed. Putting it through its paces, he backed it down the corridor and swung down as a mozo took the reins. Giving the fired-up animal a pat on the neck, he ambled back to the seats, where the onlookers were cheering. Calhoon was on his feet, pounding his one hand against his thigh. Don Diego's face still showed astonishment. But it was Bancroft's expression of dismay and envy that Tyree savored.

Calhoon embraced him. "Shan, that was beautiful! I just won a hundred dollars silver! Half of it's yours!"

Don Diego put out his hand. "Congratulations, Senor Tyree. You are one of us. Now, perhaps, you would like to try the roping—particularly the 'jerk of death?' "

"No, thanks," Tyree smiled. "I'll quit when I'm ahead." The "jerk of death" was something he had seen Alvaro do, but he had no intention of attempting it himself . . . not roping a wild mare with the other end of the *soga* tied around his neck and throwing her *without* the use of his hands.

Don Diego laughed. "Very wise." And from then on Shan sensed a subtle change in Don Diego's attitude toward the Rancho Bravo men. There was less reserve in his already flawless hospitality, and he volunteered four of his best vaqueros to accompany them as far as the Rio, as additional insurance against Apaches or other raiders.

They crossed the Rio Bravo del Norte at the San Vincente ford, where, on the Mexican side, a small presidio was some measure of protection. Ahead, on the American side, was nothing—except country apparently designed personally by the Devil himself. Jumbled bad-lands, shimmering desert, endless stretches of creosote, hills of pure gravel, the only relief in all that the towering, timber-clad hump that was the Chisos mountains. This part of the Big Bend below the Santiagos was breathtak-ing in its awesome bleakness that had a beauty of its own, but, cut by a thousand draws and washes and canyons, it offered as well a thousand opportunities for ambush by red men or white.

Calhoon, surveying it, absently stroked with his right hand the stump of his left wrist. Tyree knew all about that stump now, knew that a quarter of a pound of buck-shot bound into the leather wrapping made it a deadly blackjack in hand-to-hand fighting. "All right," he said. "We'll follow the same route back we took down—the Comanche War Trail. Hell, it's the only road there is through this mess. And we'll all have to look sharp and keep our guns handy. We've got a fortune in fine horses here that'll draw the buzzards, red, Mexican or white—"

They headed back to Rancho Bravo along the trail used for over a century by the Comanches on their raids on Mexico. Tyree saw now why Calhoon's specialty was the defense of the ranch and its property. Militarily, meticulously thorough, he organized the drive as if it were an Army operation. "There's not much grama among all this cactus and creosote and we'll graze the horses slow, keeping a tight guard on every side. Meanwhile, I want a patrol out in front of us, scouting for any sign of danger. You see any, don't try to fight. Just fire a couple of shots and burn leather back here with a report." He twisted in the saddle. "We got nine first-class men. It'll take quite a crew to get their hands on these horses without taking on more lead than maybe they want to carry."

He also assigned roving flank and rear guards. Bancroft and Tyree were to remain with the horses at all times, no matter what happened. The herd moved on at the pace of the slowest grazing mare, while each hour of shift in the angle of the sun transformed cliff and butte and canyon into different rainbow colors. . . .

Tyree rode with especial alertness. It was a strange feeling to be on guard against horse thieves instead of, on the other end of the stick, trying to figure how to take this herd. But it was a good feeling, too; good to be part of Rancho Bravo, something bigger than himself, to see some future besides the hangman's knot ahead of him, to sleep with a clear conscience. Rancho Bravo offered him everything he would ever want except— He looked at Bancroft, massive in the saddle, riding ahead, the only thing between himself and all it would take to complete his happiness—

Meanwhile, instinctively, his mind was working. How Apaches or Mexicans might operate, he could not guess, but there was no help for it—he found himself looking at this drive through the eyes of Doc Meredith and the old Shannon Tyree, who seemed no longer connected with himself. While the herd nooned on the first day, he rode to where Calhoon and Bancroft were conferring in the shadow of a huge rock.

His face must have worn a strange expression, for Calhoon looked at him quizzically. "Well, Tyree, something on your mind?"

Tyree licked his lips, hesitated. "Yes, sir. I think we're going about this drive in the wrong way."

"Are we now?" Calhoon tipped back his hat.

Aware of Bancroft's narrowed eyes on him, Tyree plunged ahead. "I been thinking about what you said, how this herd would draw a lot of buzzards, and not only Injuns. And—" He broke off, almost losing his nerve. He knew the first question Bancroft would ask when he was through. "I think the way we're drivin' now, we're playin' right into the hands of any horse thieves that might hit us. I think we ought to stop the herd durin' the day and let it graze and the men get what sleep they can and drive at night, and really push hard. On top of which, I think we got too many men concentrated around the Spanish horses and not enough around our own ridin' stock."

Calhoon's gaze shifted to the remuda, following some distance behind the Spanish stock, and herded only by one man. Every rider had a string of three horses, and there were pack mules, too, carrying supplies. It made a sizeable saddle band. Interest flared in the Carolinian's gray eyes. "Go on."

"Well, I don't know how Apaches or Mexicans might work, but . . . but I have driven a lot of horses in California, and I know how the white horse thieves work there. They wouldn't be about to hit us in daylight while we're drivin'—it would cost 'em too many men. But at night, when most of the outfit's worn out, that's when they'd strike. And they wouldn't go for the Spanish stock first off, they'd hit the cavvy. Stampede it, create surprise, a diversion—and then while a bunch of sleepy men were muddlin' around tryin' to git back on balance, they'd come after the Spanish studs and mares. Grab the whole bunch and then likely split 'em up into two or three smaller bunches and take off in different directions to rendezvous later. We'd be tryin' to get hold of our ridin' stock and even when we did, wouldn't know which trail to follow—"

Bancroft made a sound in his throat. "You sure as hell know a lot about horse thieves," he said, and there was a razor edge to his voice.

"Wait, Frank. Go ahead, Tyree."

"If we lay over in daytime, they got to come after us in bright light, and I just don't think they'd do it. Not with all these guns against 'em, especially if we pick a place where we ain't boxed in and can see for a good distance. And movin' at night—fast as we can push the horses— that keeps 'em off-balance. It would screw up their timin'. And keepin' a stronger guard around our own saddle horses would be like settin' a trap for 'em."

"This is rough country to travel at night," Bancroft growled.

"Yeah." Calhoon tapped his saddle horn thoughtfully with the stump of his left wrist. "All the same, there's sense in what Shan says. That business about runnin' off the saddle stock—I've used that myself in raids durin' the war. I was a fool not to think about it. Tyree, you take Richards and Houston and guard the remuda along with the wranglers. Keep it closed up along with the Spanish horses. Since we're at water now, we'll stay here until just before sunset—then we'll move out. Bancroft, the men can catch what sleep they can in shifts. We'll be pushin' hard after dark. And—" He grinned. "There's a trick I used once before in a situation like this. Once we move out come night time, I don't want any Rancho Bravo man wearin' hats. That way, we get hit at night, we won't be firing at our own men."

"Captain Calhoon, you mean—" Bancroft's face was dark.

"I mean we'll try it Tyree's way. Indians, Mexicans or whites—it makes sense and it ought to work."

"And maybe we'll be ridin' into an ambush in the dark. Maybe this is all a set-up."

There was silence for a moment, as Tyree and Bancroft stared at one another. Then Tyree said quietly, "Are you accusin' me of workin' with horse thieves?"

"I'm not accusing you of anything," Bancroft said after a second. "We'll see how things work out."

Calhoon put his horse between them. "Stop it, you two. I've made my decision, it's my responsibility, and that's the way it's gonna be. Now, Tyree, you get with the re-muda—"

Tyree's eyes locked with Bancroft's for a moment. Then he nodded, said, "Yes, sir," and wheeled his horse. But there was a kind of sickness within him as he rode down the line. *Bancroft knows,* he thought. *I should have kept my mouth shut and let whatever happens, happen. California ain't that far off. And he'll never be satisfied now until he digs out the truth. . . .*

*   *   *   *

It was a tricky business pushing the horses at night, even on the well-defined war trail, under a half moon. Darkness did strange things to this Big Bend wilderness, transformed it into a spooky nightmare shadowland. It made it harder to control the Spanish horses, too, which followed the natural tendency of their kind to want to turn back to their own home range. Hatless riders cursed and grumbled, bandannas wrapped around their heads to protect their ears from the chill wind. All the same Tyree, in his heart, knew the extra work was worth it. A herd settled for the night was like a flock of sitting ducks before a marksman; one on the move was a difficult, shifting target, especially with nine guns to protect it, and their owners all awake. He and Doc, Tyree thought, would have calculated the risks and shied away, unless they had overwhelming force to back them up. Thieves worked by night, expecting honest men to be asleep. They hated it when it was the other way around.

Anyhow it worked, at least for the first two nights. On the third night, they were making the final push for the gap in the Santiagos, which would bring them out on open rangeland, having encountered nothing more alarming so far than a few lobo wolves which trotted along behind the herd out of rifle shot, hoping for a stray or injured animal.

Tyree, keeping the remuda in close behind the Spanish horses, was doubly alert tonight. If there were to be trouble—from Mexicans, Apaches, or Americanos—it would most likely come before they were through the Santiagos. He hoped to God there'd be none—Calhoon then would have to give him partial credit for that, and it would give Bancroft no chance to blow off at him any farther. But if it did come and Rancho Bravo had to lose a man— No, that was a rotten thought, as much as he wanted Lacey. A shudder of desire ran through him as he remembered her lips on his, her body in his arms—

They were crossing open flats now, with the line of the Santiagos bulked against the sky ahead. A man could relax a little here, and Tyree reached for makings. He had just pulled the tobacco bag from his shirt pocket when there was a strange *clunk* almost at his groin, his whole saddle shook, and the roar of a rifle shattered the uncanny silence of the desert. Dropping the tobacco, his saddle horn shattered by the near miss, he raised his rifle—and then there was more shooting and a wild whooping and they were coming, boiling out of a draw a quarter of a mile behind and firing as they came—at least six riders—bearing down on the remuda to scatter it.

"Richards, Houston, Jones!" Tyree bawled. "Hold 'em tight!" Startled by the shooting, the horses whinnied, tried to break. Tyree spurred his mount, fought them back into a bunch while other hatless men cursed and did the same. Then, as the range closed, the gunflashes nearer, lead making its ugly whine through the darkness, Tyree and his men opened fire. It was up to them to stand off this assault, up to Calhoon, Bancroft, and the others to watch the Spanish horses.

Bent low in the saddle, he and his men pumped the levers of their rifles, shooting at the muzzle-flashes of the guns of the oncoming raiders. A horse in the remuda, hit by a stray slug, screamed, went down. Tyree cursed, sought a target, found one only a couple of hundred yards away, a sombreroed rider in the moonlight. He reined in his mount and his Henry kicked against his shoulder, and more through luck than marksmanship under these conditions he saw the man spill backward off his horse's rump. Somewhere across the herd a man cried out in pain; a pack mule brayed. Tyree hosed a triple string of shots at another muzzle flash, heard a hoarse gurgling sound. Then a man's voice yelled, "Back! Back, goddamnit. Swing and—" For a moment, Tyree's hands froze on the gun. *No!* he thought, throat dry, *it can't be!* And then there was no more time for thinking as the oncoming riders changed direction, swung back and out and wide and then forward toward the Spanish horses.

Tyree pumped a shot at a fleeting target in the moonlight, knew he missed. "Houston!" he bawled. "Richards! Stay with me! Hold the remuda!" His rifle nearly empty now, he sheathed it, pulled his handgun, and fought to keep the saddle band from stampeding.

Up ahead, around the Spanish horses, all hell and then some was exploding. The night was lit by gunfire; he heard a wild warwhoop that he knew came from Calhoon's throat, a mad ululating rebel yell. "Hiiiiiyyeeeeee! Rancho Bravo!" Then it was drowned in rifle sound, the whinnying of horses. Tyree cut off a stampeding pack mule, turned it back to the bunch, whirled his mount. The sound of hoofbeats up there was changing. That voice—the one he knew so well—yelled, "Back, damn it! Whipple's gone and— *Break it off, break it off!*" Then they were in full flight, the horse thieves, scattering, pounding off across the flat in the moonlight. Tyree heard a bellow like that of an enraged bull, saw a rider charging after them, pumping lead from his rifle as went. The attackers returned the fire, but that massive figure on the running horse paid no more attention to their shooting than as if the lead were so much rain. Tyree saw a thief topple from the saddle. Then Calhoon's voice roared out: "Bancroft! You damn fool, come back here!"

Bancroft reined in his mount so hard it reared; when it came down, he checked it, turned in the saddle, emptied his rifle at the now almost formless shapes running their horses into the distance. "Form up! Form up!" Calhoon was shouting, and Tyree yelled orders, and drove the remuda straight on into the bunch of Spanish horses ahead. Bancroft sat his mount a second longer out there on the flat, then turned and galloped back to where the Rancho Bravo men were enclosing all the horses in a tight ring of riders with reloaded guns. Suddenly, except for the whinnying and snorting of the animals, the night was silent, the drum of distant hoofbeats fading.

"By God, I got me one at least!" Bancroft's voice roared triumphantly.

"They lost a-plenty!" Calhoon snapped. "Tyree!"

"I'm here!" He rode up to Calhoon.

"You called the turn, you called the turn exactly!" Calhoon's voice was still hot with battle-lust, the jubilance of triumph. "The sonsabitches thought they'd draw us off when they hit the remuda—Anybody hurt back there?"

"We lost a horse. One of our men hollered, I think it was Richards."

"It was me," a voice groaned from the darkness. "I took a slug. Somebody help me. I'm bleedin' bad—" He appeared beside Tyree, then slumped in the saddle, hand clasped to flank. In the moonlight, Tyree could see the thick dark soddenness of his shirt.

"Easy," he said, spurred alongside, dismounted,

ground-reining his horse, reaching up for the wounded man. Richards groaned and almost fell into his arms.

"Jesus," he rasped, "it hurts. It—" His voice broke off in a strange, thick gargling, and he was dead before Tyree could lower him to the ground.

⚹ Chapter 8 ⚹

Chewing on his pipe, Elias Whitton listened grimly as Calhoon recounted what had happened. Henry Gannon stood with thumbs hooked in gunbelt, all the humor gone from his homely, freckled face. Philip Killraine drummed his fingers steadily on the desk he sat behind in the Rancho Bravo office. Bancroft, lounging in one corner, watched Tyree, who leaned against the wall, face expressionless.

"Well, there it is," Calhoon finished. "There must have been about a dozen of 'em. Come mornin', we found four dead and one dyin' out on the flat. He was too far gone to tell us anything. The rest of them had hauled their freight. It was just like Tyree said it would be—they hit the remuda first, hoping that would draw us back from the Spanish stock. But when it didn't work, they ran into a hornet's nest. Anyhow, the ground wasn't right for them, the terrain. They must have been desperate to make their try before we got across the Santiagos. We buried Richards decently and dumped some rocks on the others. Then we drove fast and hard for the home ranch and made it without any more trouble."

"Only," Henry Gannon said quietly, "they killed a Rancho Bravo man."

Philip Killraine stood up from behind his desk. "And so," he cut in, black eyes hard, mustache bristling, "we must find the bastards and take them, even if we have to hunt them straight down to hell itself. No matter what it costs, we've got to show everybody in this country—Rancho Bravo avenges its own."

"Yes," Gannon said. He turned to Whitton. "Elias?"

"Three days," Whitton said. "The sign be faint, but it still be there, even allowin' two more days for us to git back to where it happened. Maybe we won't have to go that far. Likely they've already come through the War Trail gap. 'Lessn they like holin' up down yonder and playin' hide and seek with the Apaches." He took his pipe from his mouth. "I'll find their trail," he said. "I want ten of the best fightin' men we got, and I'll do the rest."

Bancroft stepped forward. "Count me in."

"No, not you," Elias said. "You married, got a kid. You took risks enough already. We got ten men with no families."

"You're married too."

"But I'm a owner. That make it different. Ten single men. Tyree, you'll do for a starter."

"He's had a hard trip already," Calhoon cut in.

"I know. If he don't want to come, that be all right.

But it look like—" Whitton's eyes met his "—he got a good idea of how these horse thief gangs work. Might come in handy. Tyree?"

Shannon Tyree stood there for one frozen instant, not knowing what to do. Ever since he'd heard that voice bawling in the darkness during the attack, he'd been sick to his very gut. Now there was no doubt in his mind that the black man would do exactly what he said. He'd seen Whitton in action; with his Comanche training, he could track a fly across a glass windowpane, and with no rain due at this season of the year, he'd pick up the gang's trail, all right, and run it down. All eyes in the room were on him now, and he knew that Bancroft was no longer the only one to smell a rat; Elias had also caught that scent. And if he were along when Elias, as he surely would, caught Doc Meredith, more than likely Doc would betray him, if not deliberately, by some act or gesture. Then he would be in the soup as well—or maybe even in a noose.

He had one salvation, one only. To refuse to go, and then, while Elias was on the hunt, leave Rancho Bravo, on the sly, forever. Goddamn him! he thought, meaning Doc, the owner of that unmistakable voice. Why didn't he stay in Colorado, Kansas, wherever— Because to leave Rancho Bravo was to leave Lacey Bancroft, to leave all the dreams that he had built. . . .

All this time, without realizing it, he was rolling a cigarette. Then, hardly realizing what he was saying, he heard himself answer: "Sure. I'll go." And stood there trying to mask his own amazement at the words. But even if it meant risking a hangman's rope, he found, he could not leave either this ranch or the woman or his dreams.

"Of course I'll go, too," Calhoon said. "It's my job." And no one quarreled with that.

"Then we pull out come daybreak tomorrow on the best horses we got. Loosh, you pick the other men."

"And don't come back without the bastards," Philip Killraine snapped.

"No," Gannon said coldly. "Don't you bring 'em back. When you find 'em, you hang 'em. Hang 'em high as Haman and leave 'em for the buzzards to pick clean—and as a warnin' to anybody else who thinks he can make war on Rancho Bravo."

The next morning they rode, not slowing until they neared the Santiagos. Then, approaching the War Trail gap, Whitton told the rest to go into camp and wait. "I may be a hour, I may be a day. I be back as soon as possible."

"You look out they don't take you by surprise," Calhoon warned.

Whitton stared at him a minute, grinned. "I don't think that hardly likely," he said, mounted and galloped off.

A full twenty-four hours passed, and somehow Tyree bore their passage. All he could think was that now Doc and his outfit had that much more head start. Surely, even if Elias cut their trail, there would be no catching them now. He began to feel better, more confident. Doc was no amateur—and not even Rancho Bravo could work miracles.

Near ten the next morning, Elias trotted his mount into camp. Shannon Tyree's confidence ebbed at the look of triumph on his face. Whitton swung down, dragged a hand across his sweaty countenance. "After they missed their chance, they didn't hang around down there in them badlands. They come through the gap, seven, eight of 'em as I read the sign. Then they split up. Three took off on their own, we got to let them go. But four of 'em stuck together, headed east. Them the ones we want."

"They've got nearly a week's start on us," Calhoon said.

"Yeah. They be ridin' like hell, maybe, the first two days. Then they figure they in the clear, slow down, git careless about coverin' their tracks. We find 'em all right," Elias said. "We find 'em if they go clear to San Antone. I think we better mount and ride."

The sign led northeast, into the high rolling grasslands of the Marathon plateau. At first Elias had to travel almost at a snail's pace, horse at a walk, himself leaning from the saddle, pausing often to cast in circles like a hunting hound. Tyree's hopes grew. Every moment's delay would put Doc and his gang that much farther out of their reach.

But no matter how many times he lost it, Elias always found the track again. A gob of tobacco juice spat into the grass, long since dried, yet a brown stain like nothing else, the scratchmarks of horseshoe calks on rock ... Once he shook his head in admiration. "I say this, their bossman know what he doing. Been in this business a long time, I reckon. But four riders can't pass nowhere together without leavin' some sort of sign—especially when they white men."

And then his pace quickened and there was jubilance in his voice. "Now they gittin' overconfident. They think they done made a clean gitaway. They never come up again' an outfit like Rancho Bravo before!" And soon he was riding at a trot, then at a lope. "Hell," he said once, "it like a wagon road now!" And that was true; Tyree and all the others could read the tracks plainly, save once when a great herd of buffalo had crossed them, blotting out the trail. But Elias only laughed at that. "They done scouted this country. We pick up the trail again at Devil Spring. They got to head for water."

And he was right. *You fools*, Tyree thought. Because they had camped there a full two days, resting their mounts, themselves, and costing themselves that much lead. But Rancho Bravo paused there only long enough to drink, then was once more in the saddle. A day later, Elias slowed. "We catchin' up fast. Got to be careful we don't overrun 'em." Standing in his stirrups, he surveyed the terrain ahead, broken by humped buttes and sandy draws. "There another spring yonderway; the Injuns call it Water Where The Wild Pigs Drink. Lots of javelinas use it. Looks to me like these jokers know about it. Loosh—" He stared inquiringly at Calhoon.

The Carolinian sat his mount thoughtfully for a moment, then nodded. "All right. I think it's worth the gamble. How far is it, Elias?"

"We can be in position come nightfall," Whitton said. He clamped down on his pipe. "There two big cottonwoods there. Jest right for what we need."

Calhoon nodded. "All right. We'll take it easy. Hang back until well after midnight, then move in."

Now, leaving the trail, they rode swiftly but warily cross-country, Whitton guiding. At twilight, he raised his hand in the signal to rein in. Resting their horses, they rode on now at a slow, careful walk into broken country. Another halt and Whitton swung down. "Now we wait," he said.

Men rolled up in blankets, snatched what sleep they could. For Tyree, there was none. All he could think of was that by daybreak Rancho Bravo would have Doc Meredith—and then his secret would be out. If he could have, he might have slipped from his bed, ridden away then and there, but, with a man guarding the horses, that was impossible. Of course, Doc was not the one to let himself be taken easily; maybe there would be a gunfight. If he could punch a bullet into Doc before he had a chance to talk— Tyree shook his head, grunted in his throat, the idea filling him with revulsion. Of course if Doc shot at him, it would be different. Anyhow, in his heart, he knew there would be no gunfight. Whitton and Calhoon had planned too well. They would catch Doc and the others cold.

The early hours of the night crawled by. Then Whitton was moving among the men. "All right. On your feet." They mounted, rode another mile or so, and then once more the black man checked them.

"Now," he said, "me, Calhoon, and five good men. The rest stay with the horses. Tyree, Nelson, Pitt, Jones, Hewitt . . . Take off your spurs and everything that might rattle. Empty yo' pockets of anything that'll jingle and take off your hats. Watch where you put yo' feet, and no talkin' whatsoever. We gonna move as quiet as little mice. They ain't but a mile ahead, if I'm right, and that we cover on foot."

Tyree's gut knotted as they made their way single-file, noiseless as a septet of shadows, down a dry wash toward a pair of buttes looming not far away, where, Elias said, there was water—and the two cottonwoods that would serve as hanging trees. The wind was in their favor, and there was no chance of the horses of anyone camped down there catching their scent and giving alarm.

It took them nearly forty minutes to cover most of that distance, through an increasing growth of low, thorned brush. Presently Whitton halted, gestured. Calhoon nodded, tapped Tyree on the shoulder, then Pitt, and the three of them climbed silently out of the draw and moved off to the right. Elias and the other two continued on their way.

Tyree's mind was made up, now, and even if there had been an alternative, he would not have taken it. During that soundless journey, his milling thoughts had settled down to grim decision. Once he had been one thing, but now he was something else—a part of Rancho Bravo. And, Doc Meredith or no, that was what he would remain. Whatever Doc said about him, he would not deny—because he was no longer the same man that he had been. The hell with his past—he had risked his life for Rancho Bravo, played more than his part in saving the Spanish horses. Calhoon, Whitton—none of them could fault him since he had hired on with the brand, and he was not the only man, he guessed, who had left a past behind him to sign on with Rancho Bravo. So, if it came down to that, let Doc do his worst, and he would take his chances, and if it came to guns, if he had to draw down on Meredith, Doc was just another enemy of Rancho Bravo. It had to be that way.

Then Calhoon halted. In the shadow of the butte, he went forward in a crouch, presently turned, beckoning the others to follow. They went quickly, silently, as their leader had done, and then they saw them: the four figures rolled in blankets around the glowing embers of a dying fire beneath the pair of giant cottonwoods, only a hundred yards away.

Calhoon waited. After a moment, from the left, an owl hooted softly. Calhoon signaled with his rifle, and, guns ready, the men walked forward. Beyond, Whitton and the others appeared from the shadows on the far side of camp.

None of the sleeping figures stirred. The Rancho Bravo men walked straight in among them, and when each man was covered by a rifle aimed point-blank, Calhoon kicked one of the sleepers gently. The man muttered, sat up. Tyree saw his jaw drop, his gummy eyes open wide at the sight of the rifle barrel pointed at his face.

"All right," Calhoon said harshly in a voice that carried. "On your feet, all of you. You're in the hands of Rancho Bravo, and the first man that reaches for a gun is dead!"

The man at whom Tyree's gun pointed stirred. Then, throwing back the blankets, he sat up straight.

Tyree sucked in a long breath. Doc Meredith looked up at him with silky blond hair ruffled, pale blue eyes slowly filling with consciousness and then with recognition. "What the hell," he whispered. "You, friend—"

"Shut up," Tyree said harshly, his eyes meeting Doc's in the fire glow and the starlight. "Keep your mouth shut. I'm a Rancho Bravo man and I'll kill you if you reach."

For one long moment Doc's eyes flickered from Tyree's face to the gun barrel and back again. During that instant, it took all of Shan's willpower to hold the gun steady.

Memory flooded back on him; he wanted to reach out, take Doc's hand, not cover him with a gun. Then Doc's pinklipped mouth in the center of his fine-haired yellow beard closed tightly. "Okay, mister," he said quietly. "Whoever you are, I'll take your word for it." And his hands came up above his head.

Someone threw wood on the fire and it blazed high. The four men—all but Doc strangers to Tyree—were searched, their weapons gathered. Then their hands were tightly tied. Doc, standing, facing Calhoon and Elias, showed no fear. "I don't know who you folks are, but you got the wrong men. We're just ordinary riders passing through. What the hell is this all about?"

Elias said, "One of you is ridin' a horse with two nails missin' from the off front shoe. Pitt, check their mounts."

Meredith said, "There ain't no need to. That's Rogers's horse. But I don't see what that's got to do with all this." He smiled faintly. "Except we didn't have no spares and blacksmiths ain't exactly numerous out here."

There was no smile on Whitton's face. "That same horse was in a raid on Rancho Bravo stock down below the Santiagos better'n a week ago. I have done followed its trail many a mile, since I first spotted that track in the badlands. There another horse here, sorrel, I think, that overreach a little when it trot."

All the humor went out of Doc's face. "Mister, who are you?" But it was Calhoon he addressed.

"Rancho Bravo," Calhoon said. "You were part of a gang that tried to steal a band of horses we were bringing from the Rio. You killed one of our riders. That is where you made your mistake. Nobody kills a Rancho Bravo man and gets away with it."

"This is all a lot of booshwah." Doc's voice was unsteady now, though. "What do you aim to do with us?"

"Come daylight," Calhoon said, "give you a good breakfast. Then hang the four of you to those cottonwoods."

Meredith stared at him. "You can't hang four men because one of 'em's ridin' a horse with two missin' shoe nails and another has a mount that overreaches."

"Well, we aim to try. Now the four of you sit down right there by the fire and we'll take the names of your next of kin and the addresses to where you want your belongin's sent."

"No!" the man next to Meredith burst out. "No, you can't—!" Suddenly, mad with fear, he raised both bound hands, lunged at Lucius Calhoon. "You—"

Calhoon swung the stump of his left wrist. There was a sodden sound as the buckshot-loaded leather caught the man on the jaw. He dropped to his knees, head down.

"The next one tries that gets a bullet," Calhoon said. "Now, let's have the information, if there is any."

Doc looked sideways at Tyree. "There isn't any information as far as I'm concerned," he said.

"All right," Calhoon said as the rest of the Rancho Bravo men came up with the horses. "Now let's get on with it."

Exhausted from the long pursuit, the Rancho Bravo men slept soundly around the fire. Calhoon had tolled off guard duty until daylight, at this time of year still five hours away. He himself had taken the first shift of two hours. And then seemingly because he had come to rely on Tyree, "Shan, suppose you take the second watch."

"Then you wake me up," Elias said.

Tyree hesitated. "Right."

Now, rousted from his blankets in the chill night, he squatted across the fire from the prisoners, drinking a cup of coffee, but his rifle at the ready. Calhoon had rolled into his blankets; the doomed men, hands tied, were in theirs, too, in a row close to the blaze. Somehow—maybe to blot out the knowledge of what tomorrow brought, the prisoners also slept. After a while, Calhoon began to snore. That was when Doc Meredith sat up, shrugging off his blankets, huddling down into his mackinaw. He looked around at the sleeping men. Then he said, voice a whisper: "Well, friend-boy . . ."

"Doc," Tyree answered, voice low, "it's not gonna do any good—" He broke off as someone turned over; when the man's breathing was regular, he went on. "It can't."

Doc bit his lip. "You can't mean that."

"I have to mean it. I'm part of Rancho Bravo now. I told you in Nevada. I've gone straight."

Doc stared at him a moment. "By God," he said at last, incredulously, "you mean it, don't you?"

"I mean it."

Meredith's babyish face was, for a moment, without expression. Then he said, "My bad luck. I could have let your wildcat outta the bag, you know."

"I thank you for not doin' so. But there is nothin' I can do in return. Goddamn it, Doc, why didn't you stay in Colorado? Why did you come down here?"

Doc's mouth twisted. "Colorado got a little hot in a hurry. Besides, heard about this Rancho Bravo, that it was gonna have a big horse operation goin'. It sounded like pickin's. Only I never expected to find you with it. Shan." His eyes met Tyree's. "You sure?"

"I'm sure," Tyree said tonelessly.

Doc shrugged, looking at his bound hands a moment. "My bad luck, I guess. Okay, I don't hold it against you. Your trail went one way, mine another. Anyhow, I hope you get what you want, friend-boy. Maybe I should have followed you. I reckon it's too late now. Tomorrow they'll stretch my neck. From where I sit now, if I had it to do over again, I'd go straight myself."

"Doc, I wish—" Tyree began in agony.

"Don't torment yourself. Breaks of the game. I'll keep my mouth shut—and I won't hold it against you."

"Doc, I'll always be thankful."

"Sure, friend-boy." Meredith shivered. "Cold. Awful cold. Don't know whether it's the wind or whether it's just me. Anymore Arbuckles in that pot?"

Tyree poured out his own, refilled the cup, came around the fire. "Now, Doc—" He kept the rifle lined.

"Don't worry. I ain't fool enough to make a break." He cradled the cup in his hands, free below the tightly bound wrists. "Jesus, that's scaldin'—" He almost spilled it and Tyree reached out instinctively, and Doc threw the steaming coffee upward straight into his eyes and was coming up on his feet simultaneously. His head hit Shannon Tyree's jaw with stunning force, knocked Tyree back. Then Doc's booted foot lashed out, caught Tyree in the belly, and all the wind whooshed out of him and, falling backwards, he rolled to miss the fire. Gasping, he mopped his eyes, sat up, and Doc was off and running toward the horses.

Tyree dragged a sleeve across eyes burning from the scalding coffee, seized the rifle, scrambled to his feet. Doc was a weaving, shifting shape in darkness; then he halted, yanking with superhuman strength at a picket pin. In that instant Tyree's vision cleared and for a pair of seconds Doc was a stationary, easy target. Tyree lined the gun, finger closing on the trigger, but something balked it before applying that last fraction of an ounce of pressure. Two, three seconds, maybe, that paralysis endured, and Doc had the pin out by then, had dodged among the horses, then was mounted bareback, picket rope like a rein, and spurring. Tyree aimed and finally pulled the trigger. And knew before the gun went off, as Doc ducked low over the horse's neck, that he was shooting high.

Then Doc was pounding out of camp, a much harder target, and Tyree hosed off three rounds, all aimed to hit, and all near misses, and the whole outfit was coming from its blankets, Calhoon yelling, "What the hell—?"

But by then Doc Meredith had disappeared into the night. Tyree, eyes puffing shut from the scalding, heard himself babbling what had happened. Calhoon listened only briefly, snapped orders to a pair of men, was mounted then and riding. As their hoofbeats faded into the distance, Shan Tyree stood with lowered rifle, a trickle of blood from a bitten tongue oozing from his mouth, his emotions an odd mixture of hangdog guilt and sick relief. At least now Doc had a fighting chance—

"My fault," he heard himself telling Whitton. "I never should have given him that cup of coffee. . . ."

"No," Elias's voice was hard. "That was a bad mistake."

"I couldn't see to shoot—"

"All right. No use cryin' over spilt milk. Calhoon and the others git him. Now, stand over here and let's take a look at them eyes. . . ."

Dawn came cold and gray, and with it the sound of approaching horses. Tyree, vision cleared, turned from the campfire, as did every man; and he was aware of a sudden thudding of his heart. The riders came into sight, then, rounding a butte, dropped down into the hollow, and his knees went curiously weak. There were three of them—Lucius Calhoon and the two men who had accompanied him, their mounts dead-beat.

"Loosh—?"

Calhoon shook his head as he swung down, facing Whitton, his mouth set grimly. "Got clean away. You'll have to take up his trail as soon as we're through with the other business." He jerked his head toward the three remaining prisoners.

Whitton squinted at the sky. "That not so easy, I don't think. Look off there to the north. See how dark it is, feel how still the air? Weather changin'; we in for a norther, my guess, before the day over. And it gonna be a real bone-rattler. Ain't gonna be followin' nobody or travelin' nowhere until it past. We gonna lay up right here, where we got shelter, firewood, and do our best to keep ourselves from freezin'."

Calhoon looked at Tyree. "How's your eyes?"

"All right, now," Tyree said.

"That's good," Calhoon said and turned away. But by the tone of those two words, Tyree knew that something important to him had already been destroyed—the full trust of the owners of Rancho Bravo. And in that moment, if he could have done it all over, he would have pulled the trigger in the one instant when Doc Meredith had been an easy target. Or would he? Tyree rubbed his face, sucked in chill air. Well, the cards had fallen; there was nothing now but to play them as they lay.

"Have they had breakfast?" Calhoon asked. He meant the prisoners.

"A big one," Elias answered.

Calhoon said, "Well, we might as well get it over with. You men—on your feet."

The three prisoners stood up slowly, faces white as paper. One of them said haltingly, "Sir, this ain't right. You can't do this to me. I—" His voice broke. "Goddammit," he almost squealed then, and tears were running down his cheeks, "we're entitled to a trial."

"You have been tried, judged, and found guilty," Lucius Calhoon said and his voice was like ice. "You did that to yourselves when you were fool enough to raid Rancho Bravo." He paused. "I don't do this with any pleasure. I hate it. Every man here hates it. But you knew all along what it would mean if you got caught. Elias, are the ropes ready?"

Whitton gestured toward one of the big cottonwoods. From a low hanging limb they dangled, swaying in the freshening wind. "I put a regular hangman's knot in each. Hope it break their necks, not just strangle 'em slow."

"Tyree. Bridle and bring up three bare-backed horses. You, Elias, and I will handle this unpleasant duty."

Tyree looked at him and saw that this was to be his penance for letting Doc escape. "Yes, sir," he said.

"The rest of you can watch or not as you please," he

heard Calhoon tell the others as he went to carry out the order.

It was something he would remember until his own dying day. Two of the horse thieves faced their deaths with silent defiance; the third, who had already begged, came to pieces. He prayed and screamed and wet his pants and voided his bowels; and he was the one assigned to Tyree to handle. He was still blubbering as Tyree somehow wrestled him up on to the horse and led the animal beneath the dangling noose. "Oh, God," the horsethief cried, a man gaunt and slender. "Oh, God, somebody help, somebody have some mercy. . . ."

But there was no mercy in Rancho Bravo. Tyree's hands trembled on the reins of the three horses, all gathered in his hands as he stood before their heads. Calhoon and Elias, mounted, carefully adjusting the hangman's knots under the left ears of the victims, making sure each noose was tight, then reined their horses back.

"Now—and do it smartly!" Calhoon commanded.

Quickly Tyree led the horses out from beneath the doomed men.

They slid off the horses' rumps, dropped. The sudden weight and impact of the fall jerked their heads aside, and the two heavier ones died almost instantly. Not so with Tyree's man, the slender, terrified one who'd begged.

As if determined to cling to life as long as possible, he kicked violently in a wind of gathering chill, body turning, legs flailing, face swelling, turning purple. "Tyree!" Calhoon snapped, and Shan knew immediately what he had to do. Running to the dangling man who stank of his own excrement, he seized both legs, clung tightly, then fell down, adding his own weight. Above him there was a faint crackling sound. The horse thief's head lolled to one side and suddenly the legs were motionless. Tyree let out a gasp of relief, backed away. The three corpses, all motionless, rotated slowly in the freshening wind. Moving aside a pair of steps, Tyree vomited until only dry heaving racked his body.

Calhoon's own voice was thick. "So we missed one. But this norther will take care of him—without blankets and equipment, he hasn't got a chance. Now leave the bodies where they are, and let's get the camp ready to ride out the storm. Tyree, you did well."

Chapter 9

The norther lasted for three days, and it was brutal. The temperature dropped with incredible swiftness; snow mixed with sleet came boiling and howling across the high range. With ample firewood, blankets, and the lee of the buttes for protection, the men of Rancho Bravo rode it out well enough, though towards the end their rations began running short. The three bodies dangling from the cottonwoods became shapeless, ice-caked lumps. Tyree, huddled in his sugans, thought of Doc out there in the open, without even a saddle blanket for shelter, his pockets emptied of everything they held, no match in his possession to light a fire. That he could survive this was impossible; he would have died easier if he had let himself be hanged. And yet, Tyree was glad that he had escaped. However Doc Meredith died, he himself bore no guilt in the killing of him, and remembering the strangling man whose neck he'd had to break, that was a vast relief to him.

Meanwhile, he was once more a fully accepted member of Rancho Bravo. *You did well.* That accolade from Lucius Calhoon had meant the restoration of the faith of the owners in him. There were no recriminations from anyone about his letting Doc get the best of him. So now once more he had a future, and, riding out the blizzard, he planned it. Once back at the home ranch, he'd really bear down now. But God, he'd work from can to can't to make Frank Bancroft look like an amateur alongside him, he'd give Whitton and the others no choice at all but to take the horse division away from Bancroft, give it to him. And Lacey— Somehow he was going to get her, too. If he could push Bancroft hard enough, make him fight, take risks, to keep his authority ... The man, anyhow, was over-age for a bronc twister; that was a young man's game. Sooner or later, if you rode too many rank horses, your number came up, and a man in his late thirties like Bancroft could, like a pitcher, only go to the well so often before being broken beyond repair. As the wind howled around the buttes, it all came clear in his mind. Not by spring, maybe, not even by summer—but by a year from now, he'd have rawhided Bancroft until the man would be lucky to be alive. It dawned on him that it was murder he was plotting—murder by outlaw horse. For a moment something in him recoiled. Then he told himself that Bancroft had hired on to handle wild ones. And if he couldn't do it, if he was over the hill, that wasn't Shan Tyree's fault.

The norther ended, as quickly as it had come. Overnight, the weather changed, and an almost springlike warmth descended on the land, the accumulated snow melting quickly. Rancho Bravo saddled and rode, leaving behind the three bodies dangling from the cottonwood. . . .

But more bad weather lay ahead. A number of the Rancho Bravo riders decided to draw their pay, head for Fort Sumner, Santa Fe, El Paso del Norte, any town where they could have a spree, promising to return early in the spring. For the others, long stretches in line shacks lay ahead, to ride out the occasional storms and turn back any cattle drifting ahead of them. For those on the home ranch, there was comparative inactivity, although the owners used every device to keep them busy—idle men had time to quarrel and start trouble. For the four owners of the ranch, it was a time to plan—and Bancroft and Tyree, to his satisfaction, were drawn into the planning.

"First thing is," Elias said, "we want to keep them Spanish horses in close where we can keep an eye on 'em. Cain't pamper 'em, but they got to winter over at least one season before they can run loose and take care of themselves up here. We'll wanta keep 'em pretty well close herded on that south range where the broken country makes a kinda barrier and where there's plenty of canyons to give 'em shelter. And they'll have to be checked on a couple of times a week to make sure they're weatherin' out the winter okay."

"I'll see to it," Bancroft answered. The easy authority in his voice raised Tyree's hackles, but he was careful to give no sign.

"Now, let's talk about next year," Killraine said. "For

an operation that's just getting under way, the horse division has done most satisfactorily. I think we ought to consider not doubling, but tripling its operations next year. The capital's available to hire the men, set up more breaking corrals, holding pens and stables down-canyon next spring and get it to standing on its own two feet. With you in overall charge, Elias, and two good men like Bancroft and Tyree to ramrod the operations—"

Bancroft froze. "Now, wait a minute, Captain Killraine. What's this about Tyree ramrodding anything? When I signed on here, the deal was that I took orders from Elias and otherwise I had a free hand. If I want an extra ramrod, I'll pick my own!"

Something jumped exultantly in Tyree, but he said nothing. Killraine looked up at Bancroft in surprise from behind the desk. "All right, ease off, Frank. It was just a suggestion that made sense to me if we expand the way I think we ought to. . . ."

Whitton arose from his chair. "Awright, that my mistake. It ought to been me that put it to Frank. But, Frank, we've done some talkin' and—" He gestured. "This whole territory is pressed down and runnin' over with wild horses, all the way from the Pecos to New Mexico, from the Rio to the Colorado. The day of the Comanches and the Apaches ridin' free is about done. I've talked to the Comanches about it and even they admit it. They don't care how many horses we take, long as we leave enough for them. There hundreds, thousands, of mustangs out there, and they Rancho Bravo's meat. But they ain't gonna last forever. There be other mustangers comin' in, and sooner or later other ranchers that'll shoot 'em down to save the graze. We got to git 'em while we can. The market for broke horses growin' every day—the Army, the ranches back east that drive up to Kansas now, Colorado, New Mexico—it's about to boom. Not to mention what we got to have ourselves. This is somethin' that's gonna be a hell of a lot bigger than we figgered on, and we got to set up to handle it. Come spring, we got to put together crews of mustangers to round up the wild ones, and we got to have a bunch of stompers to break 'em out. Ain't no two men, you and me, can handle and oversee everything. That why we kinda figured on splittin' the ramrod's job. When we hire you, we didn't figure on a man of Tyree's caliber showin' up, too, and it makes sense to put him to the best use. We calculated to put you in charge of the mustangin' and him in charge of the breakin'. But that don't in no way put you down. He gits a raise—but we aimed to cut you in for five percent of the profits."

For a moment there was silence in the room. Bancroft's square face had turned a bright red, his lips thinning. Tyree tried not to change expression, but already he was thinking: *And he'll be gone most of the time and I'll be here with Lacey—* Then Bancroft said, "What you mean is, you like Tyree's way of breakin' horses better than mine."

No one answered for a second, and that interval was answer enough. Then Whitton said gently, "Frank, let's face it. You gittin' a little along in years for snappin' out the wild ones. You and me the same age, about, and I know how it feel to me when I ride a real bucker now. It don't take but a few years of that to tear loose ever'thing a man's got inside of him. You've rid your share. You owe it to your wife and kid to ease off before you git too busted up."

"I can ride any goddamn horse Tyree can!" Bancroft exploded.

"It ain't just one horse, it dozens over and over."

"Maybe," Bancroft said thinly. "But all the same—"

"All the same what?" Tyree, temper rising, spoke for the first time.

Bancroft whirled on him. "All right, you want to make me say it. The boys told me about how he let that damned horse thief git away out yonder. And they told me something else—that of all of 'em, he was the only one ridin' a *Californio* rig! And Tyree's made a big show of bein' a *Californio!*"

Blood burnt in Shan's cheeks. So Bancroft anyhow had guessed. He took a quick step forward, the best defense a strong offense. "You sayin' I was in with that bunch, let him go deliberately?" His eyes met Bancroft's, and he had forced a ring of steely anger into his voice.

Bancroft stood there like a bull half-decided to charge its enemy, right hand dropping low to his holstered gun. "I'm sayin' this. On the way up from Mexico you knew exactly how they'd hit us. Then, when the outfit caught 'em, you let the big dog get loose, and him from the same place as yourself. I'm sayin' you know an awful lot about how horse thieves operate for a man that's never been one himself!"

Tyree sucked in breath. "That's bad mouth to lay on any man, Bancroft. I could call you out for that."

"You do that," Bancroft rasped. "I've gone thirty-eight years sayin' what I think. I ain't stoppin' now."

Tyree's own hand swung low. He'd seen Bancroft at

the mandatory target practice that was part of Rancho Bravo's routine, knew the man was fast on the draw, accurate in his aim. But no faster, no surer, then himself: Doc had taught him well. And now, he thought, maybe this was his chance—

Then Gannon was in between them, eyes blazing, hands on his own gun butts. "Enough of this! Frank, you're out of line—way out of line, unless you got some proof. You're callin' Tyree a horse thief. What you got to back it up?"

"I only said—" Bancroft broke off, groping for words. Then he shook his head, and his shoulders slumped, and Tyree knew why. A few more words would have made Rancho Bravo too small for both of them, and Bancroft suddenly feared that given a choice between Tyree and himself, the owners might choose Tyree.

"No," he ended and his voice had changed. "No, I'm not accusin' him of anything. What I said was ill-spoken, and I make Tyree my apology." But the words were grudging.

Tyree hesitated. Gannon would not let it come to gun play, and unless Tyree accepted Bancroft's apology, one would surely have to leave—which meant he might never see Lacey again. "All right," he said. "Forget it."

"Exactly," put in Loosh Calhoon. "Frank, if you don't like what we had in mind, we'll do more talking. Something will be worked out. Now maybe the two of you had better each go his own way while we have another pow-wow."

"Let's say, if it counts for anything, I'd rather be in charge of breaking and let Tyree do the mustanging," Bancroft said thinly, wheeled, stalked out.

The partners were silent. Tyree waited a moment, then followed Bancroft. Outside the stone fort, he watched the man cross the yard to his own house, enter, close the door behind him, and a pang shot through him. Bancroft alone in there with Lacey, possessing her. And he himself had not had a chance to touch or hold her since her husband had returned from Fort Davis. Yet, when passing, their eyes met briefly, it was all still there in hers, plain to read, her wanting of him. . . .

And, Tyree thought, a chill walking down his spine, maybe Bancroft had seen that, too. Maybe that was really why Bancroft had been about to crowd him. Well, that kind of crowding was a game two could play at, and as he went to the bunkhouse a plan was forming in his mind.

It was a fine Sunday afternoon, midwinter but warm as spring, when Tyree led the outlaw horse into the corral. Caught in the last mustang hunt, it had been a six-year-old stallion; now gelded, it still had a stud's strength and fire. But what made it a true outlaw were the long, ridged scars along its withers and its flanks. One glance at those and what had happened to the horse was plain to see: years back, a cougar had dropped off a rock or out of a tree onto its back. Somehow the horse had bucked off the mountain lion and survived, but anything that touched its back brought back a memory of terror. Bancroft and Whitton both had wanted to shoot the animal as incorrigible and useless, but Tyree had interceded. In conformation the horse was magnificent, strong and tall, but, more than that, it was a challenge, the kind he liked. If he could win its confidence, make it finally bear a rider's weight and turn it into a working animal, he would have accomplished a miracle. Meanwhile, with plenty of other animals to break, he'd left it 'til last. Now, with time on his hands, he'd had a chance to work with it.

It had, now, been put through all the preliminaries. It allowed men to approach it, had been sacked out to rid it of the tendency to shy, it would even lead. But it still would not tolerate even a saddle blanket's weight on its back. The moment anything came down there, it simply exploded.

Now Tyree had spread the word around that today he would try to ride it. Because Sunday was a day of rest on Rancho Bravo and entertainment scarce, the top rail of the corral was lined with men like buzzards on a limb, and even the women—the partners' wives and Lacey—had come out to watch. Bancroft was there, too, of course; Tyree had counted on that.

In fact the big Kansan and Elias Whitton helped him throw, tie, and saddle the animal, a violent job that left them all panting by the time the cinches were strapped. "Man," Elias gasped, stepping back, "you really think you can ride this bronc?"

"If I can't, it won't be the first time I've eaten dirt." Tyree looked mockingly at Bancroft. "I'll ride him." He seized the reins, took position, one foot in a stirrup, bent and seized the horn. "Let 'im up."

Whitton and Bancroft slipped the ropes. The gelding, already frantic from the weight of the saddle, came straight up, and when it did, Tyree was astride. His left foot caught the stirrup, and then the world was a crazy blur as, screaming, fighting to rid itself of the menace behind its withers, the horse bogged its head and turned into a hammering, twisting, soaring machine, landing with gut-smashing impact, swapping ends, grunting, pounding.

Tyree took that punishment for half a dozen jumps. After those few, he knew that he could make the ride, but it would leave him stove-up for days, which was not his plan. He deliberately let his seat loosen, lost rhythm with the bucking, and then he was going, kicking feet from stirrups. Arcing through the air, he seemed to take forever to hit, and when he did, though he tried to relax his body, it was with stunning force. Instinctively he rolled, then came scrambling to his feet, ran to get clear of the plunging animal, still fighting the saddle on its back. Panting, dazed, he made the fence, to jeers and raucous laughter—and the loudest laughing came from Frank Bancroft. "Well, you ate your dirt, Tyree!" Then, with ropes, he and Whitton were sliding off the fence. A couple of minutes more and they had the horse stretched out once more. Tyree shook his head to clear it as Bancroft's voice came jeeringly. "Wanta try another ride?"

"I—" Tyree began, but before he could find more words, Bancroft went on loudly. "Maybe I better show you how it's done. This kind of horse don't call for your fancy *Californio* stuff—what it takes is a real bronc-stomping rider!"

Tyree rubbed his face, trying not to show his exultancy. There had been a purpose in all this and Bancroft was responding exactly as he'd hoped. "You think you can take him?"

"I know I can! Pitt, you come give us a hand—"

"Frank," Elias said, "maybe you hadn't—"

"Somebody said somethin' about me bein' too old to ride. By God, I'll show you who's too old! Pitt!"

"Frank, please!" That was Lacey, fear in her voice, calling from behind the fence.

He ignored her as Pitt took one of the ropes, got himself into position just as Tyree had. And just as the horse had done before, its strength totally undiminished, when it came up, it came up fighting—with Bancroft in the saddle.

The battle it had put up against Tyree was nothing compared to the way it fought Frank Bancroft. Tyree, still aching in every joint, feeling as if all his guts were wrenched loose inside him, leaned against the fence watching as, spurs raking, quirt lashing, Bancroft made his ride.

No horse Tyree had ever seen had bucked like that. It threw itself skyward, twisted belly up to the sun at the height of its leap, recovered, came down with jolting stiffness. It swapped ends, it twisted its head and tried to bite, it pawed the air, it snapped its hind legs out and back, and still Bancroft stuck, spurs going hard, driving it to greater frenzy. Then Lacey screamed. Suddenly, without warning, the bronc reared high, teetered on its hind legs, fell backwards. Dust roiled and at first it seemed certain that Bancroft had been smashed beneath it when it hit, the saddle horn probably punched through his belly. But then the dust cleared, and Bancroft was not beneath the horse at all, but on his feet, and as it rolled, came up, he hit the saddle again and found the one stirrup he had lost. Tyree looked at Lacey. Her hands were clamped on a corral bar, her knuckles white.

There had been a moment of ugly hope when the horse went down; now, it was lost in sheer admiration as Tyree watched Bancroft ride. Slowly but perceptibly the horse was tiring, its jumps losing some of their smashing impact.

Snorting, it ran against the corral fence, hoping to scrape Bancroft loose. He jerked a leg free from stirrup, got it high enough to escape the smashing the bronc had hoped for, then found the stirrup again as the horse pinwheeled away.

Turning around and around with every jump, it kept up that pinwheeling, and Bancroft's head snapped back and forth at the end of his spine like the knot on a rope's end. His quirt popped loud and hard, his spurs kept on raking, and now he and the horse were both covered with bloody foam, and Tyree swore softly beneath his breath. The brute strength of the man was winning over the brute strength of the animal.

Then the horse gave up. No longer able to jump, it ran frantically around and around the corral. Still Bancroft lashed and spurred, and the cheers of the men on the corral deafened Tyree, and then the horse had stopped. Flanks heaving, head down, it had given everything within it and had been defeated. Bancroft lashed it with his quirt, but it would not even move.

Then Bancroft was off, in a quick jump. But the moment his feet hit the ground, his knees gave way beneath him. Whitton was in the corral in an instant, running to him, and, hands slipped beneath Bancroft's arms, helped him to his feet. Blood was running from the Kansan's nose, mouth, even his ears. He was almost, not quite, dead weight, as Elias got him to the fence.

"Frank," the black man said, "I never seen a ride like that!"

Bancroft leaned against the fence, looked at Tyree. His mouth, lips bitten, corners drooling blood, twisted in a grin as his eyes met Tyree's. "That's how it's done, *Cali-*

fornio," he gasped, and then, massively, he vomited; and half of what spewed from his mouth was blood. "Frank!" Lacey screamed as his knees gave way and Bancroft collapsed, unconscious.

"Quick, you men!" Whitton snapped. "Gimme a hand. Let's git him in the house!"

Tyree did not move, only watched as they carried Bancroft out of the corral, Lacey and his son running alongside, their faces pale. Well, he thought, it had worked; but to his surprise he felt no exultancy, only a sick regret and self-disgust.

Chapter 10

※ Chapter 10 ※

There was no moon tonight, and the wind that blew through the cottonwoods was chill, but not as cold as La-ey Bancroft's hands when Tyree took them in his own. That show-off ride had torn loose a lot of things inside Frank Bancroft; even now, forty-eight hours later, he was till in bed, under Whitton's orders to lie as quietly as possible. "He's asleep?" Tyree asked.

"Yes, but I can only stay a minute." She pulled her hands away. "Shan, did you have to put him up to that?"

"I put him up to nothing. I got thrown and he wanted o make me look like a damned fool, so he made the ride f his own free choice."

"But you knew he would." Her voice was accusing.

"I didn't know anything." He reached for her hands gain. "It's only settled one thing. When he's able to ride

again, he'll be in charge of the mustang hunting in th
spring. I'll be here to handle the bronc stomping. An
you know what that means—time together. God, I'v
missed you so much, Lacey." He bent his head, tried t
kiss her.

She turned her face away. "Not now. I . . . I've got t
think."

"Lacey, I love you—"

"I know." Her voice was thick. "I love you, too. I trie
not to, I fought it, but— Shan, we'll have to wait and see.'
Once more, she pulled away. "Now, I've got to go back t
him. He's still a sick man." And she whirled, disappeare
into the shadows.

When she was gone, Tyree cursed softly and, makin
sure he was not observed, left the grove. Once in th
clear, he lit a cigarette; the smoke had a bitter taste. Al
right, he *had* planned it and it had worked out as he'
hoped. Had let himself be thrown, knowing that the
Bancroft would not be able to resist the challenge to sho
him up, and that at his age the horse was bound to be to
much for him. He'd known that one way or the other
would put Lacey's husband out of action and the two o
them could steal some time. It had seemed to him that h
could not go another day without her in his arms.

What he had not expected was the strange backfire i
her attitude, or that she would see so easily through hi
scheme. Still: *I love you, too,* she'd said. And: *We'll hav
to wait and see.* . . . Well, there would be time enough fo
that. Bancroft's days of riding the rough string were over
when he was fit again for the saddle, he'd be gone fo
weeks at a time all through the spring and summer
mustanging, and then Lacey would come around, the

ould work things out. . . . Tyree ground out the cigarette,
ntered the ranksmelling bunkhouse full of snoring men,
olled into his own bed. But it was a long time before he
ot to sleep.

With incredible vigor, Bancroft was up and around the
next day. Somehow, to Tyree, he seemed to have
hanged. There was no gloating about having made a ride
he *Californio* couldn't, none of his blunt harshness. He
eemed strange, withdrawn and brooding. And, Tyree no-
iced, he had changed his style of wearing his revolver. It
was slung low now, and the tie-down thong that once had
angled loosely was fastened around his thigh, gunfighter
style. At odd times during the next two days, in which
they hardly spoke, Tyree would become aware of Bancroft following him with his eyes, and they were cold,
metallic. A kind of warning bell rang in Tyree's head.

On the third day, Bancroft spoke directly to him for
the first time. Shan was sitting on a bench before the
bunkhouse, making a new hackamore, when he saw Bancroft coming toward him. Instinctively he laid aside the
rope, shifted weight. Something in Bancroft's bearing
made him want his gun where he could reach it, and as
Bancroft planted himself before him, Tyree stood up.

Bancroft's eyes raked him up and down a moment. But
what the man said was not what a suddenly tense Tyree
expected. "You checked those Spanish horses lately?"

"Yesterday," Tyree said. "They're all there."

"Well, saddle up," Bancroft said. "We're gonna check
'em again today."

"*We?*"

"You and me."

"You're in no shape to make a ride that long."

Bancroft stared at him oddly. "I," he said tonelessly, "am in shape to do any God damned thing I have to do. Now get your horse."

"I told you I just checked—"

"And I told you we're checking them again. Nobody's told me yet that I'm not still boss of this division and that you're not working for me. You coming or you ain't? If you ain't, draw your pay and ride." Before Tyree could answer, he turned away, striding toward the corral. Watching him go, Tyree felt his stomach knot. There was really no need to check the Spanish horses again today. Bancroft had some far different purpose in mind, and— *All right,* Tyree thought. *So if he's found out and wants a showdown, maybe it's just as well it comes to a head right now.* Hitching at his gunbelt, he carefully hung up the half-finished hackamore and followed.

The range of the Spanish horses was two hours' ride from headquarters, sheltered valley land hemmed in by rough breaks that formed a natural barrier to keep the animals from drifting south. The first hour of the ride was made in total silence, Bancroft's face grimly set, Tyree tense as the string of a drawn bow. He noticed, however, that Bancroft had chosen the horse with the easiest gait in his string, and that even so the slightest stumble or misstep made the Kansan's face flicker with pain. You had to hand it to the man, Tyree thought: he was not only a superb bronc stomper, but he was all guts.

After an hour, in the shade of a mesquite thicket, Bancroft, without warning, reined in his mount, swung down.

Tyree halted his own horse. "You see? Even an hour and you got to rest. You head on back, I'll check the horses."

"No," Bancroft said, standing there spraddle-legged. "Git down. I want to talk to you."

Tyree stared at him a second, then swung off, ground-reining his horse. His stance matched Bancroft's own, alert, ready for anything.

The wind ruffled the branches of the thicket. Somewhere in the distance, a cow bawled. "All right," Shan said. "Suppose you tell me what's on your mind."

"A lot of things. But we'll start with Lacey."

Tyree kept his face expressionless. "I don't see what you're drivin' at." But, as Doc had taught him, he was watching Bancroft's eyes, not his gunhand. If a man drew against you, his eyes would betray him even before he reached.

Bancroft licked his lips. "You know what I'm drivin' at. You're ten years younger than me and so is she. I knew when she married me, it wasn't for love; she had to have a man that would look after her. Well, in these past years, I've done my best to do that—and hoped she'd ..." He groped for words. "Hoped she'd come to feel about me, like I do about her. I thought she had—until you came along."

"Bancroft—"

"Be quiet. Sometimes I'm a little slow to catch on. But I've seen the way she looks at you, and then the other night— She thought I was asleep when she slipped out of the house. Well, I wasn't. And I got a pretty good idea of where she went and who she saw."

"All right. If you want to—"

"Shut up and let me finish. And take your hand away

from that gun. I ain't goin' to draw on you. God knows, I ought to, but you saved my kid from them longhorns that day and that's what's saved your own hide this far."

His voice shook a little as he went on. "Gittin' back to Lacey. There's nothin' I ever wanted for her, but for her to be happy. If I thought . . . If I thought that you could make her happy, do a better job than me, then . . . I might even stand aside. But I don't think that. Because I think that once a horse thief, always a horse thief, and that ain't the kind of man I'd ever want to see her married to."

Tyree said, "I'm a Rancho Bravo man like you. I ain't—"

"What you are now, I don't know. But I'm pretty damned sure of what you used to be. You had it all figured out how those people would hit them Spanish horses comin' back from Mexico, and when the outfit finally caught 'em, it was you that let the big dog of the bunch git away, and him a *Californio* like you. It sticks out all over you—you're just accustomed to takin' anything that strikes your fancy . . . whether it's another man's horse, his job—or his wife. All right. Maybe you're man enough to take my job. God knows, you've made a start at it. But you ain't goin' to take my wife."

He paused. "If you go straight, stay straight, play it for Rancho Bravo all the way, I'll never mention this again. But you leave my wife alone, you keep your hands off of Lacey, or I'll kill you. Now, you've had fair warnin', I've had my say, and there's an end to it. Unless you want to fight it out right now. Which won't do you any good, because if you kill me, Lacey wouldn't touch you with a ten-foot pole. I may not be all she wants, but I'm the father of her son."

He broke off, then, and only stood there looking at Tyree with cold eyes, a flicker of emotion barely crossing his face, his stance ready for anything.

Tyree sought words, found none. At last he answered, "All right. You've had your say. And I ain't about to fight it out with you right now. I wouldn't fight any man as stove up as you, and besides, we're both Rancho Bravo." Deliberately, he turned his back on Bancroft, in that moment seeing himself through the eyes of the other man. It was a pretty shabby picture, but it did not change his longing for the woman; she was in his blood. He swung up into the saddle. "You wanted to check them Spanish horses, let's get about it." And he spurred off, leaving Bancroft to follow. The other mounted, caught up with him immediately. They rode well apart from then on, not looking at one another, not a word passing between them, until at last they topped a rise and looked down into the valley in which the Spanish horses ranged.

Below them stretched the valley floor, vast, lush with good grass even at this season.

It was empty. There was not a horse in sight.

For a long moment, Bancroft, mount tightly reined, stared. So did Tyree. Then Bancroft whirled his horse. "I thought you said—"

"I did. Yesterday. They were all there—a full tally." Suddenly Tyree was cold all over. "Maybe they've ranged into the breaks."

"Breaks, hell! With a warm south wind blowin'?" Then

Bancroft had yanked his rifle from its scabbard, spurred his horse, was rocketing down the slope.

Tyree jerked his own Henry clear, sent his mount thundering after. As well as Bancroft, he knew the horses weren't in the rough country—a few might have been, but not the whole herd of mares and the two studs. There was only one way they could vanish like that overnight, and he and Bancroft both knew it. Only— *Don't let it be him!* he prayed silently as his horse raced along, overtaking Bancroft's. *He swore he'd go straight, too! Just don't let it be him!*

"You swing out to the right!" Bancroft yelled. "I'll take the left! Zigzag and cut for sign!"

Tyree turned his horse, slowed it to a trot. The valley, of course, was littered, crisscrossed, with droppings and hoofmarks, but to the experienced eye there was a difference between horses feeding and horses being driven. He cut his mount back and forth, found nothing. Then, on the wind, a shout from Bancroft came to him and he turned to see the big Kansan waving his rifle up and down. Tyree whirled his horse, rode to where Bancroft waited.

"Son of a bitch!" he exploded bitterly, staring at the ground.

It was all around them, only a few hours old—the sign of a herd rounded up and being driven in a hurry. Bancroft's face was like something hammered out of iron. "This mornin' not long before first light! They drove 'em straight into the breaks! Well, it didn't take long for your friend to get back in business!"

"I don't know who it was!" Tyree flared. "I can't tell who rides a horse from the tracks it leaves! All I know is, you'd better get on back to headquarters and round up Elias and some men while I keep on this trail!"

"Like hell I will!" Bancroft snapped. "That's four hours more start they'd have—and maybe warning, too, from you, for all I know! There ain't but four of 'em, if I read the sign aright and they can't travel too fast in this rough country. They knew the herd was checked yesterday, didn't figure on it being checked again for a couple of days! I'm goin' after 'em!" And he spurred his horse.

Tyree stared. "Bancroft!" he yelled, but it was hopeless. The man was already set on a hair trigger, beyond hearing reason—and beyond trusting Tyree, with justification. "Hell," Tyree grated. "Shape he's in, a long rough ride'll kill 'im—!" Then gigging his mount, he was thundering after Bancroft. Catching up, he rasped: "Then we go together!"

"I don't want you! You go back to Rancho Bravo—!"

"I can't help what you want! I'm comin' with you!"

They stared at one another for an instant, and there was an eyelash flicker when Tyree thought Bancroft would turn the rifle on him. But then the Kansan's face twisted and he said, "All right! Come on! We got no time to waste!"

The trail was plain as print, leading into the breaks, the thieves confident of a day or two's head start. Even so, they had pushed the horses hard, working southward toward, Tyree guessed, the badlands below the Santiagos in the deep Big Bend. Once there, it would take some doing even for Elias to find them, and there were places down there, Whitton said, where just a pair of men could stand off an army. Still, Bancroft was right. Two hard-riding men unhampered by a herd had a chance of overtaking them before daylight faded. What happened then was the question.

Bancroft set a reckless pace, asking all of his horse that it would give. Down wash and draw, up ridge and over—rough riding at any time, brutal for a man whose guts had taken punishment like Bancroft's. But he never slowed, and Tyree kept pace. Once, when they paused to rest the mounts, Tyree said, "Bancroft, you're gonna bleed inside you keep this up."

"I'm all right," The Kansan said tersely. "All wrapped tight around the belly. Don't you worry about me. Now, let's go."

They took off again, and with every mile they covered, the trail was growing fresher, too fresh, it seemed to Shan Tyree, for the headlong pace at which they followed it. As, ahead, it led into a narrow canyon jumbled with rocks and brush, the rims piled high with boulders providing fine cover for anyone who watched the rustlers' backtrail, Tyree snapped: "Bancroft! Hold it!"

Checking his mount, Bancroft stared at him.

"We don't wanta overrun 'em," Tyree said. "They'll have hell's own time workin' those horses through that canyon. Rate we're goin', we're liable to come up on 'em unexpected and—"

"Good!" Bancroft snapped the single word and was off again, leaving Tyree with open mouth. "Damned fool!" Tyree grated, and rode after.

And now they were in the canyon, and despite the fact that the terrain was even rougher, Bancroft pushed his mount harder, risking falls. The canyon walls closed in around them and Tyree kept a wary eye on them. Just one rifleman up there—

But it was not from the rimrock that a shot came. Lead spanged off of rock with a nasty whine, followed by a rifle's crack. "Down!" Tyree yelled and he was off his horse and hunting cover. Again, as Bancroft leaped from the saddle, the rifle sounded, and smoke rose from a nest of boulders two hundred yards ahead, on the canyon floor. Tyree dived behind a rock, saw Bancroft sprawl on a patch of sand behind a clump of brush, roll, rifle coming to his shoulder.

"Shan!" The voice roared the words from the nest of boulders. "You crazy fool! Turn back! I don't want to kill you!"

Tyree's hands tightened on the rifle. *So it was him, all right.* A dry, hot bitter rage rose in him. "If you don't turn loose those Spanish horses, you're gonna have to!"

"Now, listen, friend-boy, you know me better than that! We rode together a damn long time—"

"So I was right!" Tyree turned his head to see Bancroft staring at him with triumphant eyes.

"Yeah, you were right!" Tyree rasped. "But what I was before don't count. I'm Rancho Bravo now and— Doc, you go to hell, you hear? Straight to hell!" The shouted words echoed in the canyon and Tyree loosed off half his rifle's load at that nest of boulders. Doc was invisible, but maybe a ricochet would flush him out—

It didn't, and Tyree crammed more rounds into the rifle. "Listen," he yelled at Bancroft. "Pump lead at them rocks. Cover me. I'm gonna—" But he was too late. As he'd been shooting, Bancroft, the same idea in mind was already on his feet, running toward the boulders, firing the Henry from the hip as he went. Tyree swore, unloosed another spray of lead. Return fire came from the rocks—and then, as if slammed by a giant hand, Bancroft went hurtling back, to land sprawled, unmoving, on the canyon floor.

"One down, friend-boy!" Doc yelled. "Don't you come after me or you'll get the same!" He pumped two more shots over Tyree's head, and then the canyon was silent. Doc, Tyree knew, had left his cover, mounted, fled. He heard the fading drum of hoofbeats.

That wild and reckless killing rage was still within him. Springing to his feet, he ran after his own horse, which, steady under fire, was where he left it. But with one foot in the stirrup, he remembered Bancroft. Swinging up, he rode to where the man lay sprawled, dropped from the saddle.

Bancroft was still alive, eyes wide but blinking, mouth open, dribbling blood. His whole shirt front was a red soddenness. Tyree whipped out his knife, cut away the cloth, saw the small hole in Bancroft's chest. Each time Bancroft breathed, a bloody froth bubbled from it.

Bancroft's voice was a whisper. "How bad—?"

"Plenty," Tyree said thickly.

"Then you git ... what you want ... after all, you damned ... thief ..." Bancroft closed his eyes.

Unconscious now, but he still breathed. Shannon Tyree got to his feet, stood looking down at Bancroft, hands knotted into fists. And now, he thought, Bancroft was right. All he had to do was wait—a few minutes, an hour—and he would have it all: the horse division, Lacey, all he'd ever dreamed of. All he had to do was let

Bancroft die. And no one could blame him, no one would ever know the truth. . . .

Time seemed to cease, stand still. Bancroft's breathing was a slow, tortuous rasp.

Then Shannon Tyree snarled an obscenity. He could not do it. What was it he had yelled at Doc? *I'm Rancho Bravo now*— Well, he was: either that or nothing. And so was Bancroft, and one Rancho Bravo man could not stand by and see another die like that without at least trying to help. . . . Tyree dropped to his knees, ripping off his shirt.

The bullet had, he judged, smashed a rib, nicked a lung. The wound would bleed internally, and there was only so much he could do, but he did it all. First, he opened Bancroft's mouth, pulled free his almost swallowed tongue, so that what blood escaped could come out orally. Then, as best he could, he plugged the wound, bandaging it with his shirt torn into strips. After that, he dragged Bancroft to the shade, then worked swiftly. He had to hunt several minutes before he found junipers the right size to yield the two long poles he needed. Quickly he lashed cross-pieces between them, wove a network of rope, fastened his blanket from his saddle roll, and then he had a travois to drag behind the Kansan's horse. As gently as he could, he laid Bancroft in place on it, tied him to keep him from rolling off. Then, mounting, leading Bancroft's animal with the travois dragging, he struck out for Rancho Bravo.

It was fortunate for Bancroft that shock kept him unconscious. Working out of the breaks was a slow, brutally rough process, the travois slipping, jarring, although

Tyree chose the easiest path he could. From time to time, he dismounted, checked the wounded man. Blood continued to trickle from Bancroft's mouth, but with incredible tenacity he clung to life.

It seemed to Tyree that was the longest journey he had ever made. Time was of the essence, and yet he dared not jar the wounded man too much. He forgot Lacey, forgot his ambitions, his whole focus now was on the ground, the quickest, easiest path back to Rancho Bravo, and on getting Bancroft there alive.

Then, at last, they were out of the breaks, and Tyree sponged Bancroft's face with water, sopped up some of the dribbled blood with his bandana, and, remounting, struck a faster pace, keeping to level ground as much as possible. Still, a purple twilight bathed the land and ages seemed to have slipped by before, at last, he saw ahead of him in the wide canyon, the lighted lamps of Rancho Bravo. Then a guard challenged him and he yelled the news and a shot was fired; and like ants from a kicked-over hill, the rest of the Rancho Bravo men were coming to his aid.

※ Chapter 11 ※

He threw away the empty tobacco sack, opened a fresh one, rolled another cigarette, mouth stinging from the chain-smoking of the past two hours. There was no room for him inside the little house where Whitton and Killraine, who served as the doctors of Rancho Bravo, labored over the wounded Bancroft. Lacey was in there, too, helping them; and meanwhile, there was nothing for him to do but wait outside, while his own life hung in the balance. He had done all he could for Bancroft; if the man died now, his conscience was clear—and everything that had belonged to Bancroft was his for the taking.

And yet, curiously, he found himself hoping for the man's survival. He had invested so much care, attention, so much of himself, in getting Bancroft back here alive—

Torn both ways, he drew in smoke that burned his throat. Damn it, how much longer would they be?

Once alerted, they'd wasted no time in getting the man to bed. Killraine had a complete set of surgical instruments, and they'd had to probe for the bullet. Meanwhile, Gannon and Calhoon had questioned him—and he had told them far from everything. The quarrel between himself and Bancroft was not their business, and when Gannon had asked, "You got any idea who the horse thieves were?" the answer had stuck in his throat. Finally it had come out, "No."

And that, at once, he knew was a mistake. Because Bancroft, if he lived and talked, could prove him a liar. And then he would be deeper into the hot grease. They would wring the reason for his lie from him, and then he would be through at Rancho Bravo.

He threw the cigarette into the yard, a spark-shedding arc of redness. So he should be wishing Bancroft dead long since—and, turning, looking into the lighted window, he thought: *Maybe he is.* Which did not mean that he was through with Doc Meredith. Not by a long shot. He had given Doc a chance, the extra pair of seconds when he could have pulled the trigger that night beneath the cottonwoods, that had made all the difference of life or death to the man. And this was how Doc had repaid him.

Oh, he could understand. Just the thought of those Spanish horses had been more than Doc could bear. Knowing they were there on the Rancho Bravo range had set him to drooling like a hungry wolf at the sight of a young heifer, and he had no more been able to help himself than a stalking, starving lobo would have. He knew the feeling, all right—and yet it was not right for Doc to come back to prey on Rancho Bravo. It was— Then he turned, as the door opened and Lacey Bancroft came out.

"Shan," she said, voice hoarse.

He went to her, took her hand.

"He'll live," she whispered. "Elias says he'll live, thank God." And then, for a moment, she sagged against him and he put his arm around her.

In that instant, he himself did not know what he felt— sick disappointment, relief all mingled, emotions he could not sort out. But when she pulled away, there was no doubt of hers. Lamplight struck her face and, drawn as it was, it was radiant, almost transfigured.

"Lacey—"

"Everything's different now." Her voice was low; she spoke almost as if she were in a dream. "He never talked before, he never said . . . how much he loved me. But in there just now, he told me. How much I meant to him, how much *we* meant to him, his wife and son. He said . . . he said all the things he never could find words for before. And, Shan— Shan, darling, I was wrong."

"Wrong?" The single word came hoarsely.

"It was all wrong, you and me. I was bored and he worked so hard and we were apart so much. . . . But I can see it now, what a . . . a tremendous man he is, how hard he's worked for us, how much he's sacrificed for us. We're his whole life, he said. Everything that means anything to him . . . And I feel the same way about him. When I thought he was dying, I knew it. I knew that if he died, something in me would die with him. But he won't die now, and we'll live, we'll both live, Frank and I. Together. Always."

"I see," Tyree said, a sickness in his belly.

"So it's over," she whispered. "I'll always be grateful to you for bringing him back to me, but it is over. . . ." She pressed his hand between both of hers, brushed his lips with hers, whispered, "I owe you a debt I can never pay," and then went back inside.

Tyree stood there motionless, mouth twisted. And yet, for all the hurt he felt, it seemed to him a weight had lifted from his shoulders. Without even knowing that he did it, he rolled another cigarette, mind gone blank.

Then they were there, stepping out on the porch, the partners of Rancho Bravo: Gannon, Killraine, Calhoon and Whitton. "Tyree," said Henry Gannon. He closed the door behind them. "We want to talk to you." In the darkness, Tyree could not see his face.

"Yeah?" Shan took the cigarette from his mouth.

"You lied to us," said Gannon. "You told us you didn't know who the horse thieves were. But Bancroft was able to talk a little. He said the one that shot him called you by name, warned you back. Even yelled that you had ridden together long before." Gannon paused. "It was Meredith, wasn't it? The one you let escape the last time."

Tyree was quiet for a pair of seconds. Then he said, "Yes."

"Before you came here," Killraine said in clipped tones, "you and he rode together. You were horse thieves, weren't you?"

Tyree did not answer.

"All right," Calhoon said. "What you were or weren't doesn't matter. That's the thing about Rancho Bravo. But it's what you are now that does. And we aren't sure what you are."

"Bancroft," Elias cut in, "says you're Rancho Bravo. He says that if he dies you ought to be the man that heads the horse division. But us, we got a different notion. He lyin' in there bad shot up, our Spanish horses gone, and all because you let that Meredith git away last time. That don't sound to us like no man to head anything."

As he spoke, Calhoon had moved around behind Tyree, and suddenly there was the hard, cold roundness of a gun's muzzle in Tyree's back. "So take off your gunbelt," he said. "You're gonna be locked up for a while. Until we get those Spanish horses back and catch that Meredith and make him talk. And if it turns out you were in cahoots with him, God have mercy on your soul; you'll hang, like him."

"I wasn't," Tyree said, standing absolutely rigid. "Let me ride with you, I'll prove it."

"You rode with us last time and we know what happened. Now, take off that gunbelt. You're goin' in the lock-up. And if it turns out we don't get those Spanish horses back or if Bancroft dies, you've got a lot to account for. Maybe enough to hang you."

Tyree looked at their faces: Henry Gannon, Philip Killraine, Elias Whitton. There was no mercy in any of them; only conviction that he'd reverted to type, that he and Doc were still working together. Bringing in Bancroft hadn't offset that; he'd done the damage to himself when he'd lied about not knowing who the rustlers were.

And so there was nothing for it but to unbuckle the gunbelt and drop it. Elias searched him, took his knife. "Move along," Calhoon said, and with a gun at his back marched him to the jail.

There were times on Rancho Bravo when men had to be locked up. The jail consisted of a small house built of stone, its walls going deep into the ground below the hardpacked earth. It held a cot, one bucket for water, another serving as a toilet, and the door was of oaken slabs, strapped with iron, fastened with a heavy padlock. It slammed behind Tyree with a sound of finality. Here he would stay until they made up their minds to free him— or to hang him.

Wearily he stretched out on the cot. Whether Bancroft lived or died, all his dreams were gone now, like so many soap bubbles pricked by fate. Maybe he'd been a fool even to try to go straight. Maybe you could no more outrun your past than you could outrun your shadow. But . . . damn Doc Meredith! Damn him to hell! Tyree sat up quickly, the hatred of his former friend that welled up in him too strong and bitter to leave him motionless. He began to pace the tiny room. If he ever met Doc face to face again— Savagely he struck the wooden door with one clenched fist, as if it were Doc himself; and the pain in his hand felt almost good.

Then he heard them: riders pounding past the jail, a lot of them. Rancho Bravo was already in pursuit; by daylight, they'd have reached the canyon where the fight had taken place, pick up the trail from there—and then God help Doc Meredith! Tyree swallowed hard, wrenched by a great yearning to be part of that band thundering past, part of Rancho Bravo once again. But, of course, there was no hope of that—ever. As the hoofbeats faded, he sank back on the cot, and presently, utterly discouraged, fell into a kind of doze.

How long he lay there he had no way of knowing, nor

even what awakened him. But suddenly he was sitting up, aroused by a faint sound. By the time he was on his feet, it came again, an almost inaudible rattling at the door.

Tyree tensed, fists clenched, ready for anything. Long seconds passed as he held his breath. Then, only a few inches, the door swung open. "Shan?"

"Lacey!" he blurted in astonishment.

"Shhh. Be very quiet!" she whispered, and then she had slipped inside, closing the door behind her. He could barely see her in the faint moonlight lancing in through the place's single tiny window set high up in the wall. "Lacey," he breathed, going to her. "What—?"

Her voice, almost inaudible, shook a little. "I stole the key. It wasn't hard—they keep duplicates in the main house and I slipped in. . . . And this—" She held out something to him in the darkness and when he took it, he felt the good, familiar heft of Colt and cartridge belt. "It's Frank's," she went on. "And his best horse is just down the canyon, under the cotton-woods. His spare rifle, blankets, everything you'll need behind the saddle."

The gun already buckled on, he went to her and took her arm, something beginning to lift within him. "Lacey, honey—"

"No. Don't." She wrenched away. "But . . . I heard them talking, and it was talk I couldn't stand—of hanging you. I won't let them do that. I made up my mind."

"Then you still love me." To him that was all that counted.

She hesitated. "I guess I do, in a way. I guess I always will, but that doesn't matter. It's too late for that now, and besides, I love Frank more. But . . . Shan, there's no time for talk. You have to go, and you must hurry.

You've got to get past the guard at the end of the canyon And . . . please. Don't ever come back."

After an instant, Tyree said, "If that's what you want."

"It has to be what I want."

"All right. But you'll be in trouble. . . ."

"No one will harm me. I'll simply tell them—you saved my son and then you saved my husband and I would not let them hang you. I'll have no trouble—it's you that has to worry. Right now everybody's asleep but that guard down there. If you walk your horse . . ."

"Yes. Don't worry about me. I'll get by him."

They stood for a moment, very close to one another, wordlessly. Then she was in his arms, and he held her tightly. Her lips brushed his, but only briefly. "Now, Shan, for God's sake, run!" She pulled away.

For one second more he stood there. Then he said, "I'm gone," and with his hand on gunbutt edged out the door. He did not even look back as he ran silently, zigzagging through the shadows, until he reached the horse.

Perhaps the guard drowsed a little; maybe it was that he walked the horse through shadows, knowing that end of the canyon well. Anyhow, he was finally in the clear, open country stretching ahead of him beneath a quarter moon. Then he put the horse into a hard, fast lope, turning it southeastward.

She had chosen well; it was a fine animal, with speed and bottom, and as its gait devoured ground, Tyree fought down the turmoil within him and made his plans. It would cost time and his endurance and the animal's, but in the long run it would be the shortest way: an end-run around the broken country, a bypass of the rugged canyon in which he and Bancroft had fought the horse thieves. If he rode hard all night, took his chances in the daylight, maybe, just maybe, he could get ahead of the Rancho Bravo men and hold his lead. Then a swing back to the west and surely he would cut the trail somewhere along the line of the Spanish horses. . . .

When dawn came, he was riding through rougher country now, the southeastern edge of the stretch of badlands, where they tapered off. Somewhere behind him, in the rocky canyon, Whitton would just be picking up the trail. For a man like him, it would be so plain that he, too, could follow it at top speed, and he knew the country even better than did Tyree. But he had several disadvantages on which Tyree counted. Meredith had turned to fight, having learned his lesson, keeping a close eye on his backtrail now, and Whitton would have to be wary of running into another ambush, losing more valued men; that would slow him down. So would the sheer number of riders with him, no matter how good their mounts. A posse like that one could only travel at the speed of its worst horse or worst horseman: one man alone, like Tyree, with a superb animal and knowing how to get the most out of it, could outdistance such a group. So he had a chance, a fair one anyhow, of getting and staying ahead of Rancho Bravo.

Besides, he knew Doc Meredith. Doc knew that Rancho Bravo was on his trail again, and this time there would be no dallying along the way. He would push those Spanish horses for everything they had in them—and if he used a tactic he had used before, might even drop one or two of the worst ones off as he went. Rancho Bravo would have to stop to pick them up, and that would give Doc a further edge.

A three-way horse race, Tyree thought. Doc and his men ahead of him, hampered by the stolen herd, himself in the middle, hampered by nothing, Rancho Bravo coming hard behind, yet slowed by the need for caution. That made him the nut between the jaws of the cracker—but that was not something he cared about right now. All he cared about was finding Doc Meredith first. When he did, somehow he would settle all accounts, make Doc pay, and besides that nothing else mattered. It was Doc he wanted, and as long as he got him, he did not care what happened to himself. Everything he had ever cared a damn about was gone and so it made no difference. . . .

Meanwhile, his concern was for the horse. He must get from it every ounce of speed and strength it could yield, yet not exhaust it. Half his concentration was for the course he took, the other half for the big bay gelding. He was sensitive to every nuance of its pace, the pumping of the lungs in its barrel beneath his thighs, the pounding of its heart, the way it took the pressures on the bit. By now it was part of himself; and when it had to rest, he let it, regardless of his own impatience—but not for one minute more than it really needed. Mostly he kept it at that steady lope; sometimes he walked it; occasionally he spurred it to a gallop. And by midmorning, south of the breaks, it was still going strong when he struck the day-old trail of the Spanish horses.

He read it with satisfaction. Doc was pushing hard, all right, but mares big with foal could only go so fast. Those were the ones he would soon start dropping off. The stallions would give trouble when Doc did that, cause further delay, but Doc would not give up the studs. Neither would he let any of the fine mares that could keep the pace drop out. And Tyree's guess was right—the trail led straight for the Santiagos: Doc was seeking refuge in the deep Big Bend.

Reining in, Tyree squinted along the back trail. No cloud of dust; he was still well ahead of Rancho Bravo. He grunted with satisfaction, and put the horse into a run.

Two hours later, he saw the first Spanish horse. Enormous with the foal inside her belly, she browsed disconsolately among the creosote that dotted this flat, seeking the sparse patches of grama. When she caught his horse's scent, she raised her head and nickered. Tyree rode wide of her; she tried to follow him, then gave it up, exhausted. She would be dropping that foal soon, he thought: to him it meant nothing, but to Rancho Bravo it and its mother would be important enough to stop for or at least detach one man to handle.

And now the trail was fresher. One of the studs was giving trouble, trying to quit the bunch; that had slowed them some. Tyree let his own horse breathe; if it held out, by nightfall, surely, he would overtake them. Five minutes later, he rode on. . . .

Ten miles farther on, they had left another mare. He passed her at a gallop, grinning tightly. Now the Santiagos were a blue line on the horizon. Long before they reached them, they would have to stop to water the herd; that would cost them another half hour, but himself only a couple of minutes. . . . Meanwhile he was certain he had left Rancho Bravo far behind. Four hours, five, he was at least that much ahead of them.

Yearning for sleep, he could fritter none of that lead away. More tired even than his horse, he swayed in the saddle, and it was with a kind of surprise that he realized the afternoon had passed, the sun was dropping, purple shadow creeping across the land, and a cold wind rising. Before long, darkness would veil the trail. Once black night had fallen, Rancho Bravo would halt its pursuit, wait 'til morning. Doc and his men, too, would have to rest and eat, as well as let the horses rest.

But there would be no rest for him. Tonight might be the only chance he had.

Then it was dark, and he could no longer see the trail. Still he kept the horse moving south, toward the Santiagos. Doc would push the stolen stock on well after dark, gain that much lead, then find a place to hole up and this time post a guard, not be caught by surprise. Any place he'd choose he'd make sure was impregnable. Anyhow, Tyree told himself, from now on speed counted for little, persistence and luck for everything. He slowed his horse, letting it walk a long time, entering broken country once again. Once he let it rest, for a half hour, during which, the reins tied to his wrist, he rolled up in his blankets—Bancroft's blankets—and slept. That catnap did wonders for him, and when he came awake, his head was clear.

Now there was nothing for his horse but to make the stalk, like a casting hound, patiently circling, sniffing, all senses alert. The stallions had lost two mares; the band two of its members; it would be restless and disturbed. He put his mount in wide arcs, trusting to it to find its own footing in this broken jumble of draws, canyons, and occasional creosote flats, and often he reined in to listen.

The quarter moon rose, but cast insufficient light for

trailing. He had not counted on that, anyhow. It was his own hearing and his horse's senses that must guide him now.

He rode forever, it seemed, through the darkness, making those frequent pauses. Midnight, he was certain, came and went. Then he felt the change in his horse. Jaded as it was, its head came up, its ears pricked, it snorted slightly, seeming to vibrate with new energy. Shannon Tyree held his breath, cocked his head.

Sure enough, he heard it, the whinny of a horse somewhere up there ahead and to the right. He felt his pulses quicken as he drew the rifle from its scabbard. Then he eased the reins, gave his mount its head, and let it go its own way. It took him up a draw that widened farther ahead into a narrow canyon. Rounding a turn of the wash's wall, he saw, then, the glimmering campfire light.

Christ! he thought. How many times, dead-beat and saddlesore, had he and Doc crouched around such a fire, guarding stolen horses, desperate for sleep, yet fearing to yield to it! It seemed now like a nightmare memory; what a rotten way for a human being to live. . . . His hand tightened on the rifle across his saddle.

As the wash headed up, the canyon opened out, he could see the fire clearly now, hear horses nickering beyond, restless, too weary either to feed or sleep. He reined in Bancroft's gelding.

"Doc! Doc Meredith! Halloo the camp!" His bawling shout seemed a desecration of the night. *Doc . . . camp . . . * The cliffs and hills fed it back in echo.

In shadow, Tyree waited, breath held, heart pounding.

There was no answer. After half a minute, he called again. "Doc, it's Shan Tyree! I'm alone!"

Still no answer. Seconds stretched by, became a minute. Tyree opened his mouth to yell again. Instead, he jumped as, from the wash's lip, not a dozen yards away, Doc Meredith said quietly but in a voice that carried, "All right, Shan. Don't make a move or I'll blow you out of the saddle. You understand me, friend-boy?"

❈ **Chapter 12** ❈

Shannon Tyree drew in breath, sat rigidly. His eyes searched the wash's rim, saw nothing in the tricky litter of boulders, brush, moonlight and shadow. "Easy, Doc," he said at last in a voice as quiet as that of the other. "I told you, I'm alone. Rancho Bravo's on your trail, but you've got a five, six hour lead, anyhow. They're on mine, too. They want to hang me."

"Do they now?" There was something like amusement in Doc's voice. "What for?"

"On account of you. I let you go one time. Then, in that fight, you called my name and the Rancho Bravo man with me heard it. They figure I'm in with you, and they locked me up, aimed to swing me. I managed to break out—"

"And tracked us down like a hound. What for?"

"Let me ride in. I'm cold and hungry. Then I'll tell you all about it."

A long silence. After a moment: "All right. Put away the long gun and ride on in, friend-boy. But no tricks. You're covered like with grandmaw's quilt ... all the way."

"Sure. You think I didn't expect that?" Shan put the horse forward. At the same time, above him on the wash's lip, he heard another horse walking. He rode up the draw with Doc keeping pace above. Then Doc let him get ahead, skittered his mount down behind, and they entered the canyon.

The fire was blazing higher, the three men around it up and ready, covering Tyree with rifles or six-guns as he rode into the light. Tyree kept his hands held high. Bearded, eyes sunken into their heads with weariness, one of them with a hacking cough and a nose streaming snot, they were as tired as he and on a hair trigger. Near the fire, he halted and Doc, behind him, said: "Okay, friend-boy. Now you can git down and tell us what it's all about."

Wearily, Tyree swung from the saddle. Doc, also dismounting, strode into the firelight. There was nothing babyish about his downy-bearded countenance now as he looked at Shan, and the Colt in his right hand was steady. For a moment he looked at Tyree. Then he suddenly pouched his gun. "All right. You can drop your hands. Unless you've changed an awful lot, you ain't fool enough to make a break."

"Doc," the man with the snotty nose said thickly.

"Hush," Doc said. He picked up a cup, poured some

coffee, held it out to Shan. "Least I can do," he said with a twisted smile, "is return the favor. Remember?"

"I remember." Tyree gulped the hot coffee greedily, feeling it spread new strength through him. He lowered the drained cup, set it on a campfire rock, straightened up.

"Now," Doc said, "what's this about Rancho Bravo bein' on our tail and yours too?"

"Well, it is." And Tyree told briefly his story. Because most of it was true, it came readily, with the ring of authenticity. Doc listened closely, head cocked to one side. "And so you're back on the dodge," he said at last. "Well, goddammit, you *would* go straight."

"Like you said you'd do if I let you go that night," Tyree answered.

Doc's mouth twisted in a smile. "I never took you for fool enough to believe that. Besides, you didn't think I could let them Spanish horses alone, did you? You know me better than that, friend-boy. The question is, where do you stand now?"

Tyree drew in breath. "Two jumps ahead of a hangman's noose. That's why I rode like hell to find you. Hell, I'm screwed anyway. There ain't but one way for me to go, now, and that's the old way. Besides—" He grinned, too. "You think I ain't been slobberin' over them Spanish horses?"

Doc laughed. "So you want to ride with us? That it?"

"That's it."

The laughter went away. "And if your old outfit comes against us—whose side you be on?"

"Goddammit, I tell you, they'll hang me as quick as you. Whose side *can* I be on?"

There was a long silence then while Doc eyed him strangely. "You mean the old way," he said quietly at last. "You and me together and screw the rest of the whole damned world."

"That's the way I mean it."

"Well," Doc said. Again a silence. Tyree stood tensely, knowing his life, in this instant, hung in the balance. "Well, it looks like we got to move out right away and God knows we could use an extra hand with these horses. And an extra gun against that Rancho Bravo outfit. Because I ain't lettin' myself be took, not by them, never again. Only—" His eyes glinted in the firelight. "Only, I'm sorry, friend-boy, but it won't work."

To Shan Tyree the night wind seemed very cold. He looked at Doc and the three men behind him with the guns, and he said, "Listen—"

"No. Because you're tainted. You see? You're a wolf, you run with the pack. You drop out, run with the dogs, you're never quite the same wolf again. Since that time you let me go, you've fought us again over them Spanish horses. You shouldn't have done that, Shan. It put the dog-stink on you. And the wolves can't trust a dog. They're wild and they can't trust anything that ever wore a collar. So . . . It's done, finished. You ride any way you want, but not with me."

Whatever Tyree had expected, it had not been this. "I ride—"

"You heard me. Any way you want, but not with us." Doc rubbed his face. "You are lucky. You let me go once when I know you could have dropped me. So you get out alive this time—favor for favor. Otherwise you'da been dead the minute you came into the firelight. Now, mount up and hightail outa here. From what you've told us, we've got work to do, and no time to waste."

"Doc—"

Meredith pointed at Tyree's horse, ground-hitched just outside the firelight. "Git on him and go."

Their eyes met.

"Sorry, friend-boy," Doc said coldly.

"All right," Tyree said. "If that's the way it is—" And then he turned his back on them, walked toward the horse.

But it was wrong, all wrong, and he knew it, knew Doc too well of old. It was all too easy and— He took two steps, launched himself in a dive, even as the first gun roared behind him and he heard the slap of a bullet over his head.

He hit hard, dragging his six-gun from its holster, rolling under the belly of the startled horse into the darkness beyond the fire and coming up saw Doc fire again, the expression of surprise at having missed almost comical on his rounded face. His own gun came up and bucked in his hand as Doc's bullet plowed into the grass beside his elbow, and Doc, a perfect target in the firelight dropped like a stone. Shan swung the Colt, loosed another round and the snot-nosed man flopped backwards. The other two were firing now, and he rolled again, came up behind the horse. They shot it, and it dropped, and he fell with it, and as it hit the ground fired across its saddle. One of the pair screamed and clutched his throat and whirled away, dropping his gun. The other tried to run clear of the firelight and Tyree's hand seemed to track him automatically. It was as if somebody else pulled the trigger, not he, but the man went down in a crumpled heap. Then, in the space of seconds, it was over, and everything was silent save for the whinnying of the Spanish horses and the strange sounds made by the man shot through the throat. Tyree lay there behind the dead horse shivering with reaction. Then he could bear those sounds no longer. Carefully he lined his Colt, fired once, and they ceased. The shivering kept up, uncontrollably. He could not remember how many rounds, if any, were still in the handgun, and he dropped it, pulled the Henry from the scabbard of the dead horse's saddle. His hands were shaking too much to have reloaded the six-gun anyhow.

With the rifle lined, he walked around the fallen horse. None of the bodies in the firelight moved. Instinctively, he turned toward Doc. Meredith lay face down beside the campfire, his dropped six-gun inches from his hand. Shan automatically kicked it well away. Gently, his throat seemingly tight-closed, he touched Doc with a boot toe.

And then jumped back as Meredith groaned and stirred.

The campfire was burning down. Shan Tyree kept the rifle lined on Doc with one hand, threw more wood on it with the other, and as the fuel caught and blazed, slowly, groggily, one side of his face covered with blood, Doc Meredith sat up.

Tyree stared at the red-sodden bullet rip along his scalp. Doc drew his sleeve across his eyes, touched the ripped place gingerly. "Godalmighty," he whispered. "I feel like a mule kicked me. What—?" He raised his head, and his blue eyes widened as he looked first into the bore of the Henry rifle and then into the face of the man who held it. "The others," he muttered thickly.

"Dead," Tyree answered.

"You?" Doc's jaw dropped. "*You* killed them all?"

Tyree nodded.

"I never figured you for that sort of gunman." Doc started to shake his head, then winced.

"I aimed to kill you, too." The coldness in Tyree's voice surprised even him. "But it looks like I only creased you."

"I always was a hardheaded son of a gun." Somehow Doc managed a kind of grin.

Tyree ripped off his neckerchief, threw it to him. "Wrap your head in that. It's still bleedin' a little."

"Obliged." Doc mopped the blood from his cheek, then bound the sodden rag around his scalp, still sitting cross-legged by the fire. Then he whispered as if he still could not understand it: "Dead, all dead." His voice was stronger as he asked, "How did you know—?"

"Because I know you," Tyree said. "I mean, I used to *think* I knew you, and before, maybe, you coulda got away with it. But when you hollered my name at that fight in the canyon, made it clear I used to ride with you, then I understood that I never really knew you at all. Because that was the same as backshootin' me. You were trying to destroy me then and there—after what I did for you that time before. Well, if it gives you any pleasure, you did. I had a job I liked, a better one ahead of me, a woman that I loved that maybe I could have got—and you cost me all of that and put me on the dodge again. And you didn't have to. It was meanness, pure and simple—like putting me on the spot by comin' after these Spanish horses again after I let you get away."

When Doc said nothing, he added harshly: "So back-shootin' was something I expected from you this time. And I was ready for it."

Doc sighed. "I yelled at you in the canyon to warn you off. I told you, I didn't want to have to kill you."

"That don't wash. You knew where I stood. You knew you might have to kill me when you came back for those horses. You just now tried it."

"So where does that leave us now?" Doc's eyes met his.

"Where I'm left," Tyree said quietly, "I don't know. But any horse thief knows what's gonna happen to *him* if he is taken."

Doc stared up at him, face gone suddenly pale. "Friend-boy, you're jokin'."

"No."

"Listen." Slowly, painfully, Doc got to his feet. "Listen, friend-boy. I was wrong. I said you'd run too long with the dogs to be a wolf. But—" His gesture encompassed the three dead men around the fire. "You're wolf enough all right. More wolf than I ever figured." Suddenly he was speaking rapidly, persuasively. "You say we still got a few hours start ahead of that Rancho Bravo bunch. You and me, we can do it, hell, we've done it plenty times. We can git this Spanish bunch headed south at a dead run, drop off a few more mares. . . . Once we git across the Santiagos I know a place down there they'd never find us. I scouted that whole damn badlands and— We'd split dead even. I already got a market for these horses once the heat's off, it would be a fortune for us both. Like old times, we—"

"No," Tyree said.

Doc looked into his eyes, then fell silent.

"Then you mean," he said at last, "you aim to hold me, let them come and hang me."

"No," Tyree said.

Doc's face brightened. "I knew—"

"*I* aim to hang you," Tyree said.

There was a long moment while only the crackling of the fire, the nickering of the Spanish horses in the rope corral up-canyon, broke the silence of the night.

"All right," Doc said finally. "We'll leave their horses. We'll both ride out together. And this time, I'll give you my word. I'm finished, through, in the business. I'll go straight, along with you. Straight as a string. I promise it. We'll find work at some spread, save our money, start our own horseranch. . . ."

Somehow Shannon Tyree forced himself to keep his eyes on Doc's face. "No."

"But, goddammit—" Doc was pleading now. "I promise! Friend-boy, you can't do it! You got to give me a chance! After all the years we rode together—"

"I gave you a chance," Tyree said. "Doc, it's no good. Save your breath."

"So you can choke it out of me."

"I'll do the best I can. A hangman's knot. Make it as quick as I can."

Doc swallowed. "Friend-boy, I'm beggin' now." Suddenly, surprisingly, he dropped to his knees and his voice was quavering. "I'll do anything you say, clear out, promise never to come near your Rancho Bravo, I'll . . ." Tears were streaming down his cheeks. "I'll tell 'em all how you took the four of us if you'll stand up for me, I'll go to prison for the rest of my life, I'll— Jesus, Shan, you got to have some mercy on me. You got to—" He dropped his head, whole body shaking.

And Tyree, unable to take any more, swung the rifle barrel with measured force. Doc slumped forward on his face. Carefully, then, with piggin strings from Doc's own belt, Tyree bound his hands behind his back.

Then, his own body shaking, he went to Doc's horse tethered nearby and unlatched the rope and began, by firelight, to make the noose. Since he had to wait for daylight, it was fortunate that he was too weary to think, and all feeling seemed long since burnt out of him.

Long before daylight, Doc returned to consciousness. Finding himself bound, Tyree watching him, with the rope ending in the hangman's noose coiled nearby, he said dully, "Friend-boy, you really aim to do it?"

"Yeah," Tyree said and got up to go through the horse thieves' gear. The food was scanty, but enough for two big meals for a pair of men. As he cooked, he tried not to listen to Doc—and tried not to remember either. It was surprisingly easy to shut out Doc's voice—the reasoning, the begging, the sudden screaming of curses, and then, at last, the sobbing. Doc cried like a child, which was something Tyree had never expected. Light had just begun to streak the east when he carried a plate of food and a cup of coffee to Meredith, who sat slumped, blubbering formlessly. "For God's sake," he said. "Haven't you got any nerve?"

"I never figured it would be me," Doc whimpered. "I never figured I would be the one to hang." He ate nothing, only drank the coffee. Then he raised his head. "Shan."

"Yeah."

"There's some booze in that pair of saddlebags yonder. Pour some in me, will you?"

"If it'll make it easier," Tyree said. He found the bottle, held it to Doc's lips. Doc drank long and deeply. It steadied him. Tyree took a single drink himself. More than one and all the props would be knocked from under him.

"Lemme have some more," Doc asked.

Again Tyree held the bottle to his lips. Doc took a pair of swallows, then another. The third he spat straight into Shan's face.

"That's what I think of you," he said bitterly. "When your turn comes, I hope you roast in hell."

"Hold me a place," Tyree said and straightened up and looked around. Dawn unveiled the canyon now. Trees were scarce down here. Nothing but stunted juniper grew on the canyon walls. Nothing to which a man could be hanged.

Then he saw it, the narrow finger of outjutting rock, twenty feet up on the canyon wall. Protruding outward a yard, slanting a bit skyward, it would have to serve the purpose. He looked at Doc's uneaten food.

"Sure you don't want that?"

"Christ," Doc said thickly. He shook his head.

"All right," Tyree said. "Well, it's time." He knotted two ropes together securely with a sheet bend, and then, as Doc sat trembling, fitted the hangman's noose around Doc's neck, adjusting the knot carefully under the left ear.

"There ain't no more I can say, is there?" Doc whispered.

"Nothing. You want to walk, or I got to drag you?"

Doc scrambled to his feet with some semblance of his old pride. "I'll walk." With the rope around his neck, he went unsteadily, drunkenly, to stand beneath the rock.

Tyree led up a horse, threw the joined rope up and over, dallied the other end to the mount's saddle horn. He and Doc looked at one another, and neither spoke. Tyree swung into the saddle. Then, suddenly, viciously, he gouged the horse with spurs and the animal leaped forward.

Two long strides and Tyree checked it.

Forcing himself to look back, he let out a long breath. This time the hangman's knot had done its work. There would be no need to drag Doc's legs.

Swaying at rope's end, Meredith's body was wholly limp, his head canted eerily sideways with neck cleanly broken.

"Thank God," Tyree heard himself say. Dismounting, he loosed his dally, tied the rope to a juniper, leaving Doc dangling with feet three yards above the ground. Going to the half-empty whiskey bottle, he drank deeply from it, but most of the raw whiskey spewed back up immediately. With no more strength in him, he rolled up in blankets beside the embers of the fire; within minutes he had fallen into a restless, haunted sleep. But he did not awaken until somebody rammed an ungentle boot-toe into his ribs. Opening bleary eyes, he found himself looking into the faces of Calhoon, Whitton, and all the pointed guns of nearly a dozen riders of Rancho Bravo.

Chapter 13

"On your feet," Calhoon rasped.

Still half-dazed, Tyree threw back the blankets, got up. "Listen," he said. "All right. I used to be a horse thief. Doc Meredith and I rode together, but—"

"Hush," Elias Whitton said. "You think I ain't done read the sign?" He gestured, and Tyree turned to see, like a bad dream become reality, Doc's body dangling from the rock.

"She let you out and you run 'em down," Whitton went on. "And, by God, found 'em before we did and took on all four of 'em. And you killed three and then hung the other—" He shook his head. "And he was your friend."

"No," Tyree said. "Not my friend. Just a horse thief, with some stolen stock."

"Rancho Bravo stock," Calhoon said quietly. "You risked your life to get it back, didn't you?"

"I had to. I'm a Rancho Bravo man. I mean ... I was—"

"No," Calhoon said. "Still are."

Tyree looked at the Carolinian.

"If you want to be," Calhoon said.

"Want to be—?" Tyree licked his lips. "God, yes, but—"

"We know you used to be a horse thief," Whitton said. "Me, I was a slave. First time I met Loosh, he was a little crazy, tryin' to find the man that cost him that right hand in a Yankee prison camp. Henry Gannon was a bankrupt. Some of these others worse than that. On Rancho Bravo, it don't matter what you used to be. You been told that. It what you are *now*."

"We can't afford to lose a man like you," Calhoon said. "Not after *this*." He gestured to the dangling body, the corpses on the ground, the Spanish horses rope-corraled up-canyon. "Especially with Bancroft finished."

"Finished?" Tyree could not help the hope that leaped in him. "You mean he's dead?"

"Far from it. But with all he's been through, he'll never do hard riding again. We're sending him and his family to Denver when he's well. He'll serve as our sales agent for horses up in Colorado—Denver, Pueblo, Fort Sedgwick, all the rest. Easy work without much riding—and he'll have a job as long as he lives, or as long as there's a Rancho Bravo. But somebody's got to take his place. After Elias read the sign, there wasn't any doubt. The job's yours, if you want it."

Tyree's knees went weak. "I want it," he said simply.

"Then good enough," Calhoon answered. "Now, we'll get those three men buried and—"

Wearily Tyree rubbed his face. He turned to look at the dangling body of Doc Meredith. "And what about him?"

"We leave him hanging," Calhoon said.

"I wish—"

"No. He stays there. As a warning."

After a moment, Tyree nodded. "I guess you're right." But when, riding out, he turned to look at the dangling body silhouetted against the brassy sky, something had twisted within him. Then he spurred his horse and had not looked back again.

The last stick of furniture from the small adobe house had been loaded into the high-sided covered wagon. Whitton, with the escort that would accompany it, stood by his mount. Lacey Bancroft, peering into the vehicle over its lowered tailgate, said, "I think you'd better put another quilt around that mirror."

"Yes, ma'am," a man inside the wagon said.

Frank Bancroft, bulk shrunken from his long period of recuperation, emerged from the house, holding his son by the hand. His craggy face was grave, as he strode to Shan Tyree, standing motionless, watching all this. "Tyree," he said.

"Frank."

As so often, Bancroft sought for words, and when they came, they seemed forced from him. "It's a big job you've got. Make it go. And . . . thanks." He put out his hand.

Tyree took it. "Good luck to you in Denver."

"We'll make that go, too," Bancroft said. "Just keep the horses coming."

"I will," Tyree said. "By God, I'll send you all you can sell."

"Just don't overbreak 'em," Bancroft said, and then he grinned. "They don't need to be able to read and write."

"You run your end, I'll run mine." But there was no acid in the words. Tyree bent, picked up the boy. "Frank, Junior, you mind your folks and watch what you try to dab a loop on and I'll see you in the fall."

"Shan—" The boy hugged him hard around the neck; then Tyree let him down.

"Come on, son." Bancroft took him by the hand again, led him to the wagon, hoisted him over the tailgate. Then he mounted the front wheel, settled on the seat, took the lines in his hand. "Lacey?" he called.

"In a minute, Frank." The woman turned from the wagon and came to Tyree and they looked at one another for a long moment. She took his hand, pressed it hard. Then stood on tiptoes, touched his lips with hers. "Shan," she whispered. "I hope you find her someday. I hope you will be as happy as I am." Then quickly she turned and hurried to join her husband on the wagon.

Whitton swung into the saddle. "All ready?" he called.

"All ready," Bancroft answered.

Whitton raised his hand and brought it down and put his horse into a walk. Bancroft popped the lines and the team leaned into the traces. The wagon rolled; the escort fell in alongside. Tyree watched them go until they had disappeared up-canyon. Absently, he took out makings, rolled a cigarette to hide the emptiness he felt, and somehow he managed to keep his face impassive. He smoked silently and motionlessly. When the cigarette was smoked down Tyree dropped the stub of cigarette, boot-heeled it out. There was an emptiness within him, but he understood Lacey's parting words. She had been almost the woman for him—but not quite. Nothing, he knew now, was worth having, horses or love, if you had to steal it. What mattered now was that there was a future and in that future there would be other women, and he knew what kind to look for and someday he would find the right one, all his, with no one else's claim on her. It would take time, maybe, but time was what he had at last.

"Tyree," Henry Gannon said behind him, jarring his thoughts.

He turned. "Yeah?"

"Until we can hire more twisters, it's gonna be kinda rough on you. But spring roundup's comin' and we need circle horses and some more cuttin' horses bad. You'd better pick some men to help you—a free hand, anyone you say."

"All right," Tyree said. He glanced up-canyon once again, but there was not even dust from the wagon. "Yeah, I guess I'd better get to work." And he strode toward the horse corrals, wholly his own domain now that he was part of Rancho Bravo once again.